HOLI MOLY! & OTHER STORIES

POORNIMA MANCO

For my husband, who taught me the value of laughter

•

"Always laugh when you can; it is cheap medicine. Merriment is a philosophy not well understood. It is the sunny side of existence."
Lord Byron

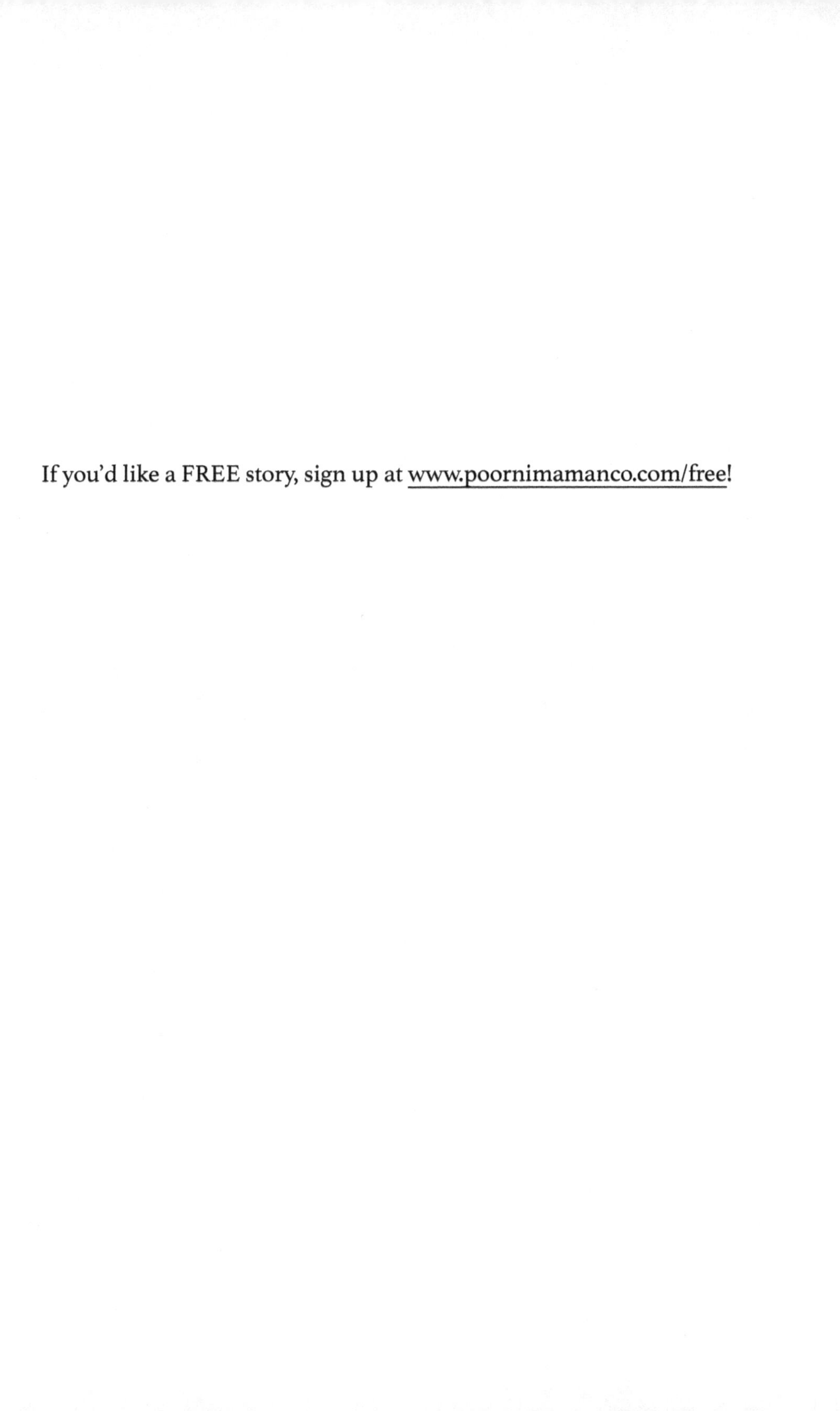

CONTENTS

1

HOLI MOLY!

"Why do *I* have to be the one?" Preeti complained, pouting mutinously.

"Because *didi*[1] is in Boston, and I am a boy!" Her brother grinned at her with his legs dangling off the edge of the sofa, knowing exactly how to irritate her further.

She scowled at him and stormed off into her bedroom to compose herself before she lost control and punched him in the face. He had been grating on her nerves for the last two years.

She missed Neeti *didi* desperately. Neeti had always been the voice of reason, the one who forestalled the rows between her and Roshan, their annoying fifteen-year-old brother, who took immense pleasure in needling Preeti, knowing she had a short fuse. Now that she was studying abroad, all her responsibilities had fallen upon Preeti, who really couldn't be bothered with the niceties of traditions and culture. She just wanted to be left alone to paint and dream of giving up her mundane career to live in a beach shack somewhere, gazing at an orange sunset with a daiquiri in her hand. Why was that so difficult for her parents to understand?

Her mother followed her into the room.

"Preeti, all I'm asking you to do is give out the invitations to our neighbours. Why are you making it this hard?"

"Mama, I'm not making it hard. I said I didn't want to do it. Get Roshan to do it. You know how long it will take, and I have work to do!"

Taking the invitations to the twenty other households that populated their apartment building didn't just mean throwing them in through the letterbox. It meant sitting through a conversation with every single aunty, uncle, *bhaiyya*[2], and budgie. They would all ask her the same questions. 'What are you doing now? Graphic designer? What is that? Does it pay well? When are you getting married?' *Didi*, ever so polite and sweet, had been really good at dodging these questions without revealing an iota of information that she didn't wish to share. Preeti, on the other hand, would either end up oversharing inadvertently or just scowl in her usual defensive manner.

"Mama, can't you see this will be a complete disaster?"

Mrs Gaekwad just raised an eyebrow at her daughter. It was enough to get Preeti to put on her slippers in a hurry, throw on a faded *dupatta*[3] over her green *kurti*[4], and put her riotous curls into a bun, sticking in a pencil to keep it in place.

"Alright, alright! I'll do it ..." She marched out of the flat muttering under her breath, "Bloody waste of time!"

In under five minutes, she had to slink back in to take the bundle of invitations from her mother's hand. Mama was not impressed.

EVERY YEAR AT *HOLI*[5], the building committee got together to organise a big party on the lawns of their apartment complex in suburban Mumbai, the hosting duties being circulated between the various buildings in the complex. With twenty-one flats in each building, the party would be a huge undertaking, with tasks being divided equally among the households. This year, their building had been appointed the task of making and distributing the invitations as Papa had a printing press and Mama was notorious for getting her RSVPs back in time. With ten days to go, Preeti had already delayed the process enough by weaselling out of delivering the invitations.

Where to begin? She eyed the broken lift and the *chowkidar*[6] sitting outside, watching the cricket match on his phone.

"*Theek kiya ki nahin*[7]*?*"

He didn't even look up as he shook his head to indicate that no, the elevator had not been fixed, and from the number of weeks it had remained in this state, she highly doubted it would be fixed anytime soon.

Sighing dramatically, she decided to take it one floor at a time, hoping that most of the residents would either be out, or at the tail end of their afternoon siestas. She'd save the best for last, knowing full well that Tasha would be back from college by then, and maybe they could sneak a smoke and a chat in the privacy of her room.

Two hours, sixteen homes, and sixteen hundred questions later, she finally made it to the top floor. Exhausted, she sat on the last step for a minute, contemplating the little spider that was crawling up the wall. A short flight of steps led to the roof terrace where as kids they'd played all manner of silly games. It had been many years since she'd come all the way up here.

She wondered if anyone ever went up to the terrace these days. Did kids even play with each other anymore, or were they just buried in video games, or whatever was trending nowadays? She thought of asking Tasha, and although Tasha's 'kids' were college-going teenagers, it was still worth getting the perspective of a teacher. Tasha made one helluva teacher, she had to admit to herself. Her badass demeanour and extensive knowledge of her subject was enough to inspire respect and admiration in her students. The fact that she couldn't care less about anyone's opinion also made her the object of much breathless adoration. Despite all that, nothing escaped her scrutiny, and they'd spent many an evening laughing over the tales she had collected in her years of teaching.

The last two envelopes sat on Preeti's lap, with her mother's beautiful calligraphy spelling out Mrs D'Souza's name on one and Mr Nanda, Tasha's dad's name on the other. She hadn't seen Hazel Aunty in years. She knew that Uncle had died of a heart attack a few years ago, but she had been away on a college trip then and by the time she got back, it was almost too late to pay that condolence visit. Mama and Papa had done the needful anyway, but a pang of guilt hit her unexpectedly. Hazel Aunty had always been so lovely to the neighbourhood kids, plying them with cakes and lemonade every time they came up to the terrace. Really, she should have checked in on her prior to this.

Preeti stood up determinedly. This time she wouldn't be grumpy and monosyllabic as with the other neighbours. She actually liked Hazel Aunty and wanted to see her. The doorbell had a pleasant chime and she waited a few minutes before pressing it again. When more than ten minutes had elapsed, she realised that the one person she'd actually looked forward to reconnecting with, wasn't in.

She tried slipping the invitation in through the recently-installed letterbox on the door. Still stiff from newness, it would not swallow the flimsy envelope she was trying to push through. Exasperated after a few attempts, she took the pencil out of her hair, letting the curls tumble down her back, and tried stuffing the envelope in with it. It took quite some pushing, as there was a fair bit of resistance from the box as well, and Preeti swore under her breath as she rammed it with all her might. With a final shove, she'd just about managed to get the entire envelope in, when a voice behind her said, "What on earth are you doing?"

Startled, her hand jerked inwards, getting caught in the steel jaws of the letterbox. Her little scream was one of surprise and pain. Her hand was stuck!

"Preeti?"

From her awkward angle she saw the silhouette of a tall, muscular figure standing atop the flight of stairs leading to the terrace. The deep baritone voice could only belong to one person, and her heart started to hammer wildly inside her chest.

"Giles? What are you doing here?"

He laughed as he descended the stairs.

"I live here, remember?"

Oh boy, did she remember! Maybe that was part of the reason she had avoided coming up here for so many years. There were just too many memories.

"Yes, but you don't live here *now*. Aren't you working in the UK?"

He had come down to her level and was staring at her quizzically. "You seem to be very well informed about my life."

"Oh, you know," she tried shrugging, still trying vainly to extract her hand from his letterbox. "Just overheard some idle chit chat from the neighbourhood aunties."

"Idle chit chat, huh? Here, let me help you with that ..."

"No!" She practically yelped when his hand touched her wrist, as though she'd been scalded.

"Hey! I'm trying to help here. Anyway, what were you doing putting your hand inside the letterbox? Trying to steal our letters?"

"Don't be daft! Why would I do that?"

"Oh, I don't know ... let me think, the last time was when you didn't want your mother to find out about your school suspension. Wasn't that when you tried stealing the letter out of your own letterbox?"

Preeti turned crimson as she remembered the incident from her childhood. His grey eyes laughed down at her, as he gripped her wrist and pulled alongside.

"I was a child," she muttered furiously, twisting her wrist this way and that. "And what is this stupid letterbox anyway? Why not have a normal one like everyone else?"

"Because, like everyone else's, that letterbox had rusted into nothing. But this isn't working. I think I'll have to unscrew the entire thing."

He drew the keys to his flat out of his pocket, while she stood there, mortified, hand trapped, sweat dripping off her brow, wondering how the hell he always managed to catch her with egg on her face!

She watched him unlock the door and open it gently.

"Wait here," he commanded, walking away from her towards one of the rooms.

Like she had another option! Why here? Why now? Why *him*?

As he walked back brandishing a screwdriver, she couldn't help but notice just how handsome he was. That chiselled jawline, those grey eyes with the ridiculously long lashes, the hair that flopped onto his forehead, his body pure muscle from years of playing cricket in boarding school. It was no wonder all the girls had swooned when he came back at eighteen, grown-up and gorgeous. All except one.

He concentrated on unscrewing the letterbox from within the doorframe.

"How's your hand feeling?"

"A bit numb," she admitted. It had only been a few minutes, but it felt like the blood supply to her fingers had been cut off for hours.

He worked away furiously while she examined him in silence. He must have known what a sensation he'd caused in the complex. The thin, shy boy, Mrs D'Souza's nerdy son, suddenly so handsome and eligible.

"So, what are you doing back here?"

"I've been posted here by my company. It's a temporary posting, just a year or two, but if I do well, then I could be promoted to running the place." He grinned up at her. "Which is what I want. I've missed Mumbai."

And Mumbai missed you, she wanted to say, but bit her lip instead.

"You didn't tell me what you were doing before I caught your hand in the cookie jar."

"Oh come on Giles! Stop implying I was thieving when you know I wasn't."

"Ha ha! Okay, fair enough. What were you trying to put in the letterbox? This? What's this?"

He'd managed to unscrew the box and gently pulled out her hand still clasped around one end of the pencil, with the crumpled envelope stuck to the other end.

Mrs D'Souza walked in just then, her plastic basket full of fresh vegetables. She looked perplexed to see her door and letterbox dismantled, and then looked up to see Preeti rubbing her swollen fingers.

"Oh my girl! Preeti, isn't it? What's happened to your hand? I just ran into your mother downstairs, she was wondering where you'd gotten to."

Giles rushed forward to take the basket from her hands.

"Mum! You walked up all those stairs with this heavy basket? Why didn't you call me?"

"Oh no, Giles, they've just fixed the lift, thank goodness. Besides, you are still jet lagged. I thought I'd let you sleep."

She turned to Preeti, smiling.

"I haven't seen you in so long. Where have you been, my girl? Here, let me ice your hand first. That looks terrible! Sit down, sit down. Giles, get the poor child a drink of water at least."

Despite her protestations, Preeti found her hand wrapped in a towel with ice cubes in it, while her left hand held a glass of water that she took little sips out of.

"What you really need is a nice cup of tea! Let me make us all some. I have some fruit cake left over from yesterday. Would you like to try some?"

Preeti nodded shyly, Hazel Aunty really was so lovely. She felt Giles' gaze upon her and fiddled with the end of her *dupatta*, still holding on to the last two envelopes, one slightly worse for wear after its trauma in the jaws of the killer letterbox.

"So, you never did tell me what all this was about?" He asked, leaning back into the armchair.

GILES WAS HER FIRST BOYFRIEND, as in, a friend who was a boy. He was smart and kind, with an emotional intelligence that allowed him to be more empathetic than any other boy she'd ever met. At first, she'd been reluctant to allow him into their close-knit group, but he'd soon won them over by his easy, ingratiating charm. Before long, they'd started swapping books and comics, inventing new games, building imaginary worlds filled with extraterrestrials and zombies that fought with sticks masquerading as guns. He was the same age as *didi*, and all of them would play quite happily together on the roof terrace, with children from the other buildings dipping in and out. When Giles found out he was being sent to a boarding school in England like his father and grandfather before him, they'd all sat together in a huddle, weeping tears of loss and despair. How cruel adults could be!

Then eight years later he'd returned, all grown up, and Preeti had fallen head over heels in love with this handsome stranger, except that he'd had eyes only for one person: her sister.

Neeti *didi* was everything that Preeti wasn't. She was tall, slim and fair, with beautifully symmetrical features, gazelle-like limbs and poker-straight hair. Always in jeans and T-shirts, she seemed not to care about her looks, which in turn, made her even more appealing. She'd lost count of how many modelling offers she'd received, or requests to participate in the Miss India contest. Neeti *didi* was just not interested. Her interest lay in books and History. If she could, she would spend entire days holed up in her college library or wandering around a museum looking at dusty artefacts.

Two years younger, Preeti was bubbly, exuberant, moody and impetuous, the perfect foil to her quieter sister. Her curls were just as bouncy as her personality, and while she had none of Neeti's classic good looks, her large, kohl-lined eyes and infectious laugh found her her own set of admirers.

But Giles wasn't amongst them.

Neeti *didi* never acknowledged his love, preferring to treat him like a little brother, just as she did Roshan. Preeti saw how much it crushed him, but what could she possibly do? Her own heart was being broken in quite the same way.

A year later, he left once again, taking his dashing good looks and bruised heart back to London. Every so often, Preeti would stalk his Facebook page in the hope that it would reveal a snippet of his life. But either he wasn't very active on social media, or his privacy settings were way too strong for her to glean anything of value from the pursuit.

. . .

THE NEXT FEW days were spent in an agony of anticipation. Would he come to the *Holi* party or not? She'd remembered seeing Hazel Aunty at a few of these gatherings, but since Preeti herself didn't care for the rambunctious nature of the festival, even though she loved parties, she would always make herself scarce after the first half hour.

He had seemed intrigued when she'd mentioned it to him. But was he intrigued enough to attend it?

Mama saw her hovering near the list of invitees that was placed on the sideboard in their living room.

"What are you doing Preeti?"

"Nothing!" She slinked away shamefacedly. It would be terrible if they found out that she was still carrying a torch for Giles. She thought she'd hidden it well enough the first time around, but *didi* had asked her gently if she was okay, after Giles had left for London. Had it been that obvious?

"YOU SILLY MOO, it was obvious to everyone!" Tasha declared this dramatically sitting cross-legged on her bed, her short bob swishing as she waved her cigarette about, scattering ash everywhere. "You'd light up like a 1000 watt bulb whenever he was around."

"Do you think he knew?"

"Him? Not a frikkin' clue! The guy was oblivious to everyone except Neeti *didi.* That was one humongous crush he had on her. Can't say I blame him. Almost all the boys were in love with her back then."

"Hmmm, true that."

"What I can't believe is that you're still crazy about him! I thought seven years would have cured you."

"Yeah, you would think," she responded glumly.

"So, what are you going to do about it?"

"Nothing. Nada. No, stop with that wicked grin, I'm just going to let it pass. Maybe seeing him again has stirred everything up, and it will all settle down in a bit."

"What, with you living in the same building? Not going to happen."

"Can you stop being so fatalistic?"

"I think you mean realistic, my pet!"

REALISTICALLY THOUGH, the probability of bumping into Giles seemed very slim. They kept totally different work hours, and even though Preeti tried varying her schedule to catch a glimpse of him, she never succeeded. In the end, she figured it was Destiny's way of telling her to give up.

As she stood at the bus-stop, letting the sea breeze ruffle her hair, she wondered if she should take up her colleague Akhil's offer of a coffee and a movie. It was a thinly disguised attempt at a date, but he had been trying for months, and something had been holding her back.

That something was honking at her from behind the wheel of his car!

"Where are you off to?"

Her heart thumping, she tried pretending complete insouciance. "Linking Road, to my office. The bus will be here any minute."

"Get in. I'm going that way, my office is in Santa Cruz."

"B ... but ..."

"Just get in, Preeti! I can't park here forever."

So she got in, hoping her trembling hands wouldn't give her nervousness away. Giles was wearing a red shirt with dark blue trousers, looking beyond movie-star handsome. She looked down at her yellow *kurti* [8]and long Aztec design skirt and sighed. Couldn't she have worn something nicer?

"What's wrong?"

"Pardon?"

"That sigh. You sounded really sad."

"What? Oh ... no, no, I was just thinking of a deadline."

"So, you enjoy all this graphic designing stuff?"

"It's not bad. I mean, I'd rather just be a painter, but the whole starving-artist thing is a tad overrated."

"Why would you starve? I remember you being very good. You painted abstracts, didn't you?"

"Mm-hm. But I think your memory might be a bit faulty. If I was that good, my work would be hanging in a gallery somewhere rather than in our storage cupboard."

"Hey, I thought you were more resilient than that? Which artist doesn't struggle? You just have to keep trying."

"Says the man in the BMW."

"Company BMW. I'm just as happy in a rickshaw or a bus. I don't even own a car in London, just get around everywhere on the tube, err, that's like the Metro there."

She turned and regarded him. "So, how are you finding being back in India after so many years?"

"I love it," he grinned at her. "After all, *dil hai Hindustani*[9]."

She smiled at him, for the first time feeling completely at ease in his company.

"Are you coming for the *Holi* party?"

"Are you?" He gave her a look she couldn't decipher. "I mean, I don't really know anyone else there, or don't remember them anyhow. It would be nice to have a bit of company."

"Yeah, I'll be there, and Tasha too. She's my best friend from the flat across ours."

"What about Neeti? Will she be there?"

SHE SHOULD HAVE KNOWN. It was never about her, never had been. The entire drive had been leading up to that one question. Dammit! She'd fumbled with her answer, watching the disappointment flit across his face before he'd plastered a polite mask on it and dropped her in front of her office.

Now she sat chewing one end of her pencil and twirling her hair around her finger, wondering how she could, once and for all, rid herself of this stupid, unrequited crush.

Akhil came and stood next to her, two mugs of tea in his hands.

"Brought you one with just half a teaspoon of sugar, the way you like it."

"Thanks Akhil, you really didn't have to."

"I wanted to." He drew up a chair and sat down next to her. "Are you alright? Seem a bit preoccupied."

"Huh? No, I'm fine. Just thinking about the *Holi* party on Sunday."

"What *Holi* party?"

An idea started to formulate in her head. She looked at Akhil, really looked at him. He wasn't bad looking, a bit on the skinny side and those glasses could be upgraded, but she wasn't perfect either, with her crazy hair and volatile temperament.

"Do you want to come?"

"Where? What are you talking about Preeti? You've lost me!"

"To the *Holi* party. It's in our complex in Bandra. We are allowed to have one extra guest per household and you can be ours. Fancy coming? There'll be food, and then we'll play *Holi* afterwards, with dry colours and *pichkaris*. No water balloons and horrid tar stuff like they do in other places. It's a very family type affair."

He watched her open-mouthed. She realised she'd been rambling on, so shut up and waited for his answer.

"Yes, I'd love to come. I guess I'll get to meet your family too?"

Oh crap! In her lightbulb moment, she'd completely forgotten that her innocent invitation to a colleague could, and probably would, be completely misconstrued by her family and the other guests. Would they think Akhil was her boyfriend? What can of worms would that open? How would they react? How would Giles react?

"WHY DOES it matter how he'll react? You want to get over him, then turn your attention to this Akhil chap. Sounds to me like he's been waiting in the wings long enough."

As usual, Tasha didn't mince her words. They were going through Preeti's wardrobe, trying to find a suitable outfit for the *Holi* party. White was a good colour to wear because once they started to play *Holi* in earnest, the multitude of colours that were flung at each other or applied gently, depending on the person, would show up very nicely on a background of white. However, all of Preeti's white shirts or *kurtis* were too flimsy to withstand the onslaught of *pichkaris*[10], which would render them transparent almost immediately.

Sitting amongst a pile of shirts, tops and *kurtis*, Preeti looked around her despondently.

"Now I don't even have an outfit to wear!"

"Ah, but I do! Benny's old *khadi*[11] shirt. It'll be quite loose on you, but it's a sturdy material and you can tie a belt around it to jazz it up."

"Won't Benny mind?"

Benny was Tasha's elder brother, who'd moved to Bengaluru with his wife and kids. Some of his clothes still lived in his parents' house with Tasha having free rein to borrow, ruin or lose as per her whims.

"Nah! He probably doesn't even remember it exists."

"What are you wearing then?"

"*Moi*? Have you ever seen me wear colour?"

Tasha only ever wore black, like some grande dame from a French Noir film. People had taken to calling her the 'Black Widow' and secretly she loved it, although ostensibly appearing too cool to be affected by other people's opinions.

"But you'll come, *na*?"

"Wouldn't miss it for the world, darling! First *Holi* party in years that the both of us are actually going to stay for."

THE DAY dawned bright and sunny, with not a cloud in the sky. Preeti groaned as Mama drew open the curtains to let the light stream in.

"Get up! I need help getting the tables and chairs set up."

"Why can't Roshan do it?"

"He is with that nice boy, Giles. They've been working for the past hour while you've been asleep."

She sat up in bed, alarmed. What time was it?

"It's 10 am. You should have been up two hours ago, but we let you sleep, you looked so exhausted last night."

"Thanks Mama! I'm sorry, I'll get ready straight away."

She slid out of bed and then paused, "By the way, a friend ... umm ... my colleague, Akhil, is also coming today. I invited him."

Her mother turned around from folding the sheet, and looked her straight in the face.

"Is there something we should know, Preeti?"

"Nope. Just a colleague."

She ran into the bathroom and shut the door behind her, but she could almost hear the cogs whirring in Mama's brain.

TASHA WAS in her usual black, but had added a colourful scarf as an acknowledgement of the occasion. *Holi* was a festival of colour, heralding the start of Spring, the victory of good over evil and celebrating the power of love and forgiveness.

In that spirit, as Preeti and Tasha walked towards the small group of organisers, Preeti decided that it was time to let go of what might have been and focus on what could be. Amongst the uncles and aunties milling about, she spotted Giles in a white T-shirt and blue jeans, looking impossibly handsome as always. Roshan was looking at him with such hero-worship in his eyes that she almost giggled at the unusual sight.

"My goodness, he's even more good looking than I remembered ..." Tasha whispered to her.

"Yes, he is, but today I'm not going to let that bother me. It's time to move on, Tash. I've decided to focus on Akhil and just get on with life, you know?"

"Smart move. So, if you're not interested, mind if I have a go?"

At Preeti's gasp, Tasha started to laugh. "Just kidding, you moo! Wanted to see your reaction, and ahem! Despite all protestations, I see that the torch still burns bright."

"Shut up! He's coming this way ..."

Giles strolled up to them, Roshan following on his heels.

"Hey ladies! Tasha, right? Preeti's told me about you, but I don't remember you from our childhood games."

"That's because I only moved here around nine years ago and we only met very briefly when you'd come home for a year."

Preeti watched Tasha bat her lids in a flirtatious manner and realised that most women just couldn't help themselves around Giles. Oh well, she was just not going to be one of them anymore.

"Is Hazel Aunty coming too?" Preeti asked, displaying a friendly albeit distant demeanour.

"Mum will join us as soon as she finishes with the giant pavlova she's making. I have to go fetch her and the pavlova in about an hour or so. We're just finishing setting up here. I hear there's going to be some entertainment?"

Preeti groaned internally. How could she have forgotten? She was meant to sing a song. In the years prior, after the song was sung, she would disappear back to the house. Nobody noticed her absence as she made herself so patently visible in the beginning, which made her later vanishing act that much easier to overlook. Now, with Giles and Akhil in the audience, she couldn't just belt out a number as imperviously as she'd always done. She'd be too nervous for that. What could she do now, after having committed to being a part of the annual performance many years ago?

"Yes, the kids in the complex normally put on a little play. Mr Bhatia does a magic act, which is really quite bad, but everyone claps and cheers for him because he's such a sweetie. Then the fat aunties get together and dance to some Hindi number, and our very own Preeti sings a song, accompanied by Roshan on his guitar." Tasha supplied all this information carelessly, although she'd never actually watched any of the performances in their entirety, preferring to sneak a smoke at those times.

"You sing too?" Giles seemed fascinated by this snippet of information.

"I'm no great shakes! Don't get your hopes up." Preeti suddenly felt annoyed, as though she was some kind of performing monkey.

. . .

The lawn had started to fill up with people and she peered into the crowd to try and spot Akhil, but he hadn't arrived yet. So, as a foursome, they made their way to the tables.

The quantity of food was astounding. People had outdone themselves in preparing all sorts of exotic dishes. *Poha*[12] sat happily next to vegetable ratatouille, chicken *biryani* next to a ham and cheese quiche, *gajar halwa*[13] next to a plum tart. There was *poori aloo*[14], *pakoras*[15], *khichdi*[16], *bhel*[17], *misal pav*[18], fish *goujons*, baked chicken, potato salad, tomato and olive pasta and more dishes than she could count. It made her head spin whilst making her mouth water.

"That's a lot of food," Giles remarked, as though reading her mind.

"Indians like their food no, *didi*?" Roshan was going out of his way to be nice to her because he wanted to impress Giles. "I hope you'll play *Holi* with us this year, Giles? *Didi* might stay if you do."

She just wanted to strangle her brother!

"Hi Preeti," Akhil's voice at her shoulder stopped her from saying something nasty to Roshan. She turned and smiled, noticing Akhil had a brand new *kurta pyjama*[19] on, with the price tag dangling off the sleeve. She held his hand and guided him away, quickly tugging the tag off.

"Sorry," she mouthed when he winced at the sharp tug. "Price tag." She held it up discreetly.

"Oh." Akhil looked nonplussed for a moment and then smiled endearingly. "I forgot to take that off."

"Who is this then?" Roshan had followed them to their quiet corner. "The 'friend' Mama mentioned?"

"Not that it's any of your beeswax, but this is my colleague Akhil." She glared at Roshan, then turned and gave Akhil her most disarming smile. "And this is my annoying younger brother, Roshan."

From the centre of the lawn, the microphone crackled alive, with the Master of Ceremonies, an elderly Mr Mukherjee going, "Testing, testing, one, two, three ..."

All the guests were invited to help themselves to the food and mingle. The function would begin after lunch, and once everyone had feasted and been suitably entertained, *Holi* would be played with the organic *gulal*[20] colours purchased by the building committee.

Tasha was laughing with Giles when Akhil and Preeti joined them, plates piled high with food.

Akhil seemed excited and was effusive in his praise. "I'm so glad you invited me here Preeti. What a lovely way to celebrate *Holi.* My part of town, these gangs wander around terrorising everybody. Most of the women stay indoors, and even the children don't play on the streets as they used to."

"Sounds rough." Giles was looking at Akhil peculiarly, as though examining an insect under the microscope.

Akhil was waving his *poori* around while expounding on his theory of why *Holi* had become such a tricky festival to celebrate.

"Is he drunk?" Tasha asked her *sotto voce.*

"What? No!" But Preeti did wonder at his garrulousness.

Soon they were chivvied along to take their seats and the children came up to perform their play on the raised platform erected in the centre of the lawn. The play was always just a variation on the themes of *Holi.* She wondered which one they'd be shown today - wicked *Holika's* burning on the pyre, her evil brother's slaying at the hands of Lord Vishnu, or Lord Shiva's return to love and life after his long meditative penance.

Turned out it was the third one, the one she enjoyed the most. Even though the performance was patchy, with the eight-year-old Shiva refusing to open his eyes while in meditation, despite the five-year-old *Kama*, the God of love, repeatedly poking him with a wooden arrow, she enjoyed it tremendously. She delighted in Giles' guffaw when it took a ten-year-old Parvati whacking Shiva on his head, to get him to acknowledge his love for her.

On her other side, Akhil had reached over to hold her hand. She wasn't sure which man was making her heart thump this hard. Torn as she was, she tried focusing on Mr Bhatia's magic tricks, but couldn't help but let her mind wander.

When Neeti *didi* had been here, they'd always stayed for the entire *Holi* shindig. Eating together, laughing together, singing together, throwing *gulal* on each other, they had been inseparable. For the first time she realised why she'd stopped enjoying *Holi.* It was because her sister wasn't around to enjoy it with her anymore.

A silent tear trickled down her cheek. She brushed it off hastily, hoping no one had noticed. Akhil held on to her right hand tightly, but it was Giles who looked at her, his eyebrows raised in question. She nodded her head, dismissing his concern, turning her attention back to the fat aunties dancing to an 'item number' on the stage. Why they chose the most ludicrous songs to dance to, no one had ever figured out, but it was good fun nevertheless to watch them wobble and jiggle.

Then it was her turn suddenly, and she stood on the stage with Roshan, the audience clapping and cheering for her.

"What do you want to sing?" He asked her, strumming his guitar. They had a little repertoire of songs they'd built up over the years: old Abba songs, a few from The Carpenters, inoffensive, sweet, melodic numbers that almost everyone knew or had heard at some point. She whispered her choice and noted Roshan's surprise. It was one they hadn't really practiced much, but they both loved the song, so he agreed readily.

She closed her eyes and let the first few notes wash over her. There was a bittersweetness to this moment. 'Killing me softly' was Neeti *didi*'s favourite song, and as she started singing, all the moments she'd spent with her sister came rushing back. Somewhere, in Boston, *didi* was about to wake up and make her first cup of coffee. She hoped that somehow her love and longing would transmit itself over 10,000 miles to her sister.

When the song came to an end, she was surprised by the thunderous applause. Roshan looked at her and grinned. "That's the best you've ever sung it. Bet your boyfriend's impressed."

Immediately her eyes sought out Giles, but he was nowhere to be seen. Instead, Akhil was clapping wildly, hooting and cheering alongside. Embarrassed, she made her way to him, but got sidetracked by people complimenting her. She'd never had a response like this before and was completely astonished by it.

By the time she made her way to Akhil, she found him corralled by Mama and Papa. He looked utterly terrified.

"So, *beta*[21], Preeti tells us you work together?" Papa was playing the good cop to Mama's bad cop routine, she could tell straight away as Mama stood by, glowering at him.

"Papa, please stop! This is neither the time nor the place. Can we just enjoy our *Holi* peacefully?"

"*Holi* isn't peaceful, girlfriend!" A fistful of colour came flying in her direction.

"Tasha! I'm going to get you for that ..."

Soon the celebrations were in full, unbridled swing with *gulal* flying everywhere, *pichkaris* being fired in all directions, colours getting soaked into everyone's skin and hair, till people became unrecognisable and shed their inhibitions totally.

There was still a level of decorum to be maintained, but Tasha, always the rebel, had managed to get her hands on some *bhang*[22]-laced *ladoos*[23] and force-fed Preeti some.

The atmosphere took on a kind of crazed feel for her. She felt happy and sad at the same time. She wondered where Giles had gone off to, then squealed with joy when Akhil, dear colour-splattered Akhil, smeared *gulal* on her cheek shyly.

The music came on quite suddenly, adding to the festive atmosphere on the lawns. People were dancing and singing together, the children chasing each other, the old ladies sitting and gossiping, occasionally allowing someone to throw coloured powder in their direction. Over the noise and the mad commotion, Akhil tried saying something to her.

"What? I can't hear you!"

He tried again, but she just shook her head. Then he took her hand and led her to the side of the building.

"What is it? What is it, Akhil?"

"Preeti ... I've been trying to tell you ... I think I'm in love with you."

The world seemed to tilt and find its balance suddenly.

She looked at Akhil and wondered what to say.

"From the moment you walked into the office, I knew you were the girl for me. Today, right here, listening to you sing, my heart was ready to explode. Preeti, I love you and I want to marry you. Please say yes!"

"Has Tasha been feeding you *ladoos*?"

He looked at her before lunging forward, grabbing her head in his hands and plunging his tongue into her mouth.

It wasn't an unpleasant feeling, but a part of her felt detached from the kiss, as though she were an observer, noticing that he tasted of *aloo sabzi*[24] and yes, a trace of *bhang!* Naughty Tasha.

She tried returning the kiss, but her heart really wasn't in it. Instead, she disentangled herself and pushed him away gently.

"I think it's time you went home Akhil."

Slightly glazed, he looked at her and then nodded slowly. He wandered off towards the building gate, and she hoped he'd make it home okay, but was too tired to follow him out and hail him a rickshaw.

SHE DIDN'T FEEL like going back onto the lawn, her euphoric mood having evaporated abruptly. Neither did she want to return home to questioning looks and vexed interrogations. She entered the lift and pressed the button for the top floor. When the lift opened on Hazel Aunty's floor, she tiptoed quietly towards the stairs that led to the terrace.

The evening breeze smelled of salt and fish. She gazed at the sea, churning in the distance, its colour like sugarcane juice, a pale khaki, rolling and roiling, wave upon wave pushing forward and retreating. The effects of the *bhang* were starting to wear off and she felt slightly stupid and weepy, all of a sudden.

"More tears?"

His voice came from a shadowy corner of the terrace.

"Giles! What are you doing here?"

"I keep having to remind you that I live here."

She turned her back on him, her emotions all over the place.

"Boyfriend's left, has he? Hence the waterworks?"

"I'm not crying!" She sniffled.

"Hey!" His voice was gentler now, closer as he came up behind her. "Everything okay?"

She turned around to face him, a sudden fury blazing in her eyes. "Why wouldn't it be?"

He backed away, wary. "You don't have to tell me anything. I'm only asking because I'm concerned, as a friend. I mean, the last I saw you, you seemed to be enjoying your tonsil-tennis with what's-his-name."

Tonsil-tennis! Where did he come up with these terms? She started to laugh, a fresh wave of *bhang* intoxication hitting her. She attacked him with sarcasm.

"Did you enjoy our *Holi* Giles, or was it all too boring for you? Is that why you left halfway through the performance?"

"I left to fetch Mum," he said quietly, "and I heard you sing. In fact, I stood near the back the entire time."

"Huh. Bet you've heard better though, haven't you? Bet you've seen better too. Prettier girls, with real fashion sense, long straight hair and ... and ... taller, yes, much taller than me ... yeah, I bet you have!"

"You're not making much sense Preeti."

"Nope, I guess not." She turned her back to him again, looking out at the sea. "Did you want Neeti *didi's* number?"

He came up behind her again. "What for?"

"To get in touch. To tell her how much you still love her."

He didn't say anything but she heard his sharp intake of breath. Then she felt his hands on her shoulders, turning her around.

"Preeti, that ship sailed seven years ago. It was puppy love, a silly infatuation, one that I believe I shared with many other boys in

Bandra. Your sister let me down gently, but she left me with no illusions whatsoever."

"Then why did you ask me about her the other day?"

"It was a polite question, like all the other questions I'd asked you that day. Why didn't you single any of those out?"

"I ... I ..." She felt at a loss for words, looking into his eyes, searching for something to say. "What's that in your hands?"

"Oh, this. A bit of *gulal*. I've been holding on to it, wanting to put some on you."

"Then why don't you?" There was a challenge and a question in her eyes.

He came closer and then took the green colouring from his hands, smearing it across her cheeks and forehead gently, his eyes boring into her, searching for something, still perplexed, wanting more.

He held his hand out. "Your turn."

She took the *gulal* and applied it on his face equally gently, her hands trembling, her heart knocking so hard against her rib cage, she wondered if he could hear it.

He stood close to her, so close that she could smell his tangy aftershave and see the beginnings of the slight growth of a beard on his chin.

Was she imagining it, or did he look ever so slightly anxious? Was the air around them really crackling with this crazy electricity? Why was he looking at her in a way that made her feel weak in the knees? His eyes seemed to be devouring her with a strange and potent intensity. All messy and filthy, covered in *Holi* colours, yet she suddenly seemed to be the only thing in the world he was focused upon.

He hesitated for a moment then, as if on an impulse, asked her, "Is that chap your boyfriend?"

"Who? Akhil? No, no, most definitely not! But why do you want to know?"

His eyes seemed to light up, a happy grin spreading across his face. He moved in even closer, trapping her between his body and the parapet. She looked up at him, all the love and yearning she'd hidden unsuccessfully all these years, written plainly on her face. Miraculously, his face seemed to mirror the same emotions.

Giles reached forward, cradling her face with one hand, the other wrapping itself in her curls.

"Because," he said, leaning in even closer, "I want you all to myself. I've been wanting to do this ever since I saw you that day with your hand trapped in our letterbox. What is it about you that has me thinking of you, night and day?" His lips brushed hers softly. "You are the most infuriatingly elusive woman I've ever encountered. Can I kiss you now?"

She nodded, closing her eyes and arching her back. Never in a million years could she have imagined Giles falling for her. Was this just a temporary crush, or could it develop into something more? She didn't know, nor did she care. It just felt so good, so *right* to be in his arms, to feel the faint bristle of his beard on her cheek, the pressure of his lips upon hers. All thoughts took flight as she returned his kiss, and as she felt herself melt into his arms, a sudden image of *didi* smiling into her coffee cup crossed her mind.

Then she forgot everything: her wet, colour-splattered shirt, the sound of the revelry on the lawns, the pink sky above her, everything except the feel of his lips and the beating of their hearts as one.

2

AN UNSUITABLE BOY

It has been said that a successful marriage requires falling in love many times, always with the same person.

Not that I would know. I have never had the occasion to fall *out* of love with my wife. Yes, we've had our fair share of disagreements and arguments. There have been times, I've suspected, that she hasn't viewed me too kindly. And three children have certainly taken their toll on our nerves, bank accounts and waistlines. Through it all though, I have loved her with a solid, some might say stolid, steadfastness.

The first question most people ask when they meet us the first time is a probing, "So how did the two of *you* meet?" It's not a polite conversation starter. It is a wide-eyed, genuinely curious query. It irritates my wife no end. More often than not, she snaps, "At University." And that's the end of that. Woe betides anyone who tries to go further.

Now, if it is me they ask, they get a different answer. The romantic in me rises to the occasion each time. I love telling our story. I love retelling it too. And since you've asked, and since we have all the time in the world while the bride and groom are sitting through their two hour wedding ceremony in the middle of the night, with the priest lecturing them on all the aspects of marriage, here we go ...

❧

To me, Sudha was as exotic as a rare bird. She was fiercely intelligent but with none of the emasculating stridency of her American contemporaries. Her kohl-lined eyes, her sun-kissed skin, her long lustrous hair hinted at an eroticism that all the perky cheerleader types in their too-tight tops and mini skirts couldn't even hope to emulate. I followed her like a helpless fool until she agreed to the first date. She told me then in no uncertain terms that it would not work. It could not work. She was Indian. I was Jewish American. The twain would never meet.

It took two years to get to the first kiss. It took another one to get her to stay over. Not once did I doubt, though, that it was worth the wait. I pined for her, I dreamt of her. She was my reason and my drug.

She laughed at my fancies and called me a fool. Then one day she didn't laugh anymore. Instead, she took my hand in hers and asked if I was ever going to make it official.

So, there I was on an Air India plane heading to New Delhi to meet the family of the girl I wanted as my wife. As per custom, I would ask her father for her hand in marriage. So far, so foolhardy.

I woke up with a jerk, feeling the roots of my hair being yanked off my head.

"Pompy!" screeched the woman behind me, "Sit down and stop pulling that man's hair!"

I half turned my head and tried to smile conspiratorially at the woman and her little monster. She ignored me while the child clambered onto the lap of the hapless man on the aisle seat. The cabin lights had been dimmed and Sudha slept peacefully by my side. I tried going back to sleep, then with a sigh plugged in my headset and turned my attention to the overhead television monitor. A voluptuous, gyrating vision swam into view. I watched fascinated as she and her moustachioed partner performed the most acrobatic of dances. Three songs and several dramatic, albeit incomprehensible scenes later, I finally nodded off, secure in the knowledge that all would be well. Indian movies always had happy endings, Sudha had once assured me.

I awoke as the seat belt sign was turned on for landing. The plump, unfriendly stewardess tartly told us off for having our seats still reclined. Chastened, we prepared ourselves for landing. Sudha's grip on my hand tightened, and I could tell that she was nervous. Very, very nervous. I gave her hand a reassuring squeeze. How bad could it be?

Nothing could have prepared me for the mass exodus from the aircraft. I was shoved and buffeted, all six feet of me, while my tiny, petite Sudha seemed to disappear into the throng. She reappeared at the door, smiling at my confusion.

The immigration officers were brusque but quick. As I waited for Sudha to clear from the Indian side of the never-ending queue, I became aware of 'the stare'. I would encounter it wherever I went over the next ten days. 'The stare' was frank and appraising, openly curious and curiously engaging.

"That's only because you're a foreigner," Sudha explained as she joined me. I tried hugging her in relief but suddenly she seemed stiff and unyielding.

"Adam, you can't touch me in public here!" she hissed.

"But why not? We're a couple. And I was only giving you a hug?!"

"This is India. PDAs are frowned upon here."

Really? I thought sourly. Who would have known it ... with a population of nearly a billion people?!

She hauled me outside. The heat, the dust and the multitude of people instantly assaulted my senses. I felt quite faint and was glad I had the trolley for support.

"There! There!! I see *Baba*," she squealed excitedly, running towards a grey-haired, tall and rangy man with close-set eyes, who beamed widely at her. Immediately, she bent down to touch his feet. He blessed her and they hugged for what seemed like the longest five minutes, I churlishly noted, given that I had been denied a hug just a few minutes ago.

Then his eyes met mine, and Delhi's heat plummeted to an Arctic chill.

"*Baba*, this is Adam. The ... uh ... friend I said I was bringing ..."

"I thought your friend was a girl," he spat out and turned on his heel.

I followed gamely, with the trolley careening wildly over the potholes while Sudha shamefacedly tried to offer further explanation.

When we got to the car park, I could barely believe my eyes. There were three members of the family waiting in the car for us. Sudha's mother, grandmother and younger brother. Where would we fit?

"Welcome to India," Sudhir, her brother whispered into my ear as I sat with my knees pressed to my chin. Sudha sat squashed next to the window, while her flatulent grandmother sat Buddha-like between us. There was pin-drop silence in the car, although the noise outside more than made up for it.

Horns blared as three-lane traffic somehow morphed into seven lanes. Cows sauntered in the midst, chewing cud blissfully, while cars, cyclists, motorbikes and scooters veered off course to prevent a collision. "Holy," whispered Sudhir again, nodding at the bovine creatures. Hawkers peddled all sorts of interesting paraphernalia at the traffic lights. Beggar children ran amok at intersections, supplicating alms with alarming efficiency. The landscape shifted and billowed from one bewildering scene to another.

We finally arrived at Sudha's house and I unsnarled myself out of the car. Our luggage was carried inside by their watchman.

I was shown to my room by her unrelenting father and asked to "freshen up" and come back out for a *chai*[1]. Tea, I soon realised, was more than just a fortifying drink, it was a bonding ritual undertaken every morning and evening in households across India.

The *chai* sat waiting with a thin film of cream, that I surreptitiously tried to push aside with my spoon. Sudha sat red-eyed in their midst as her mother kept dusting all the surfaces in the room with a manic ferocity. Only Sudhir and the grandmother seemed relaxed. One with the careless nonchalance of youth, and the other with the selfish disregard of the elderly.

"Meghna, sit down!" the father ordered and promptly the mother sat, squirming uncomfortably, looking askance at me.

"How - how long has this been going on?" her father waved vaguely in our direction.

Sudha's eyes flashed a warning to me.

"Um ... we've been seeing each other for roughly two years, sir." Although it had been longer than that, but I thought to err on the side of caution.

"And what are your intentions, my good man?"

"Intentions?"

"Yes, yes," he nodded impatiently, "Why are you here? What do you want?"

My head swam with fatigue, and I felt as though I'd unwittingly wandered into a Victorian melodrama.

"I, well, uh ... I'd like to marry your daughter, Sir."

"Marry?" he exploded. "What do you *Amreekans* know of marriage? Marry one minute, divorce the next! Meghna and I are married for twenty-nine years. My *Amma*," he said, pointing to the old lady, "for fifty years before my *Baba* died. We marry for life. Not for two minutes."

"Sir, I appreciate that, and I very much hope that our marriage will last as long as all of yours."

"Hope? What is that?? I want guarantee. Can you give me?"

I looked at Sudha helplessly. She stared back stoically.

"Hrmph!" Suddenly he tired of the conversation and waved us off to our rooms.

Bone-crunching, mind-numbing fatigue overcame me and lulled me into a sleep so deep and long that Sudhir had to shake me awake for the evening meal.

"The wolves are baying for your blood," he remarked cheerfully, as I sat up in bed disorientated. "They are all out there. They want to see this *firang*[2] Sudha *didi*[3]'s brought home."

Enter Exhibit A. I stood a foot taller than most of them. They muttered and exclaimed under their breath, but refused to acknowledge me.

Dinner was an uncomfortable affair. I attempted a few jokes to break the ice, but my American sense of humour sailed right past them. Her dad glowered at me, and Sudha sat subdued. All in all, a colossal failure.

The food was good though.

The next few days seemed to be a saturnalia of food and family. Relatives, even obscure ones, climbed out of the woodwork, to gasp at this pale giraffe, the unwelcome resident of the Agarwal household. The foreigner who had the temerity to ask for their child's hand in marriage.

I took to walking around the block for a bit of fresh air and freedom. Invariably, I'd get followed by a gaggle of kids. They'd laugh and yell, "Eh *gora*[4] Amitabh!" I figured out soon enough that they were comparing me to their onscreen idol, Amitabh Bachchan. Another tall, gangly unremarkable-looking actor whom all of India worshipped as their celluloid hero.

Evenings I'd spend in the company of the old grandma. She'd sit back and crack her betel nuts, and I'd try and read my research papers. Occasionally, she'd look at me and mouth a question. I'd smile and make my best attempts at deciphering what she was saying. Then we'd try gestures and end up laughing at each other, our non-verbal communication creating a strange but happy rapport between us.

Sudha and I had had little contact since we'd arrived. It was almost as though some (not so) mysterious forces were conspiring to keep us apart. Sudhir would intermittently deliver messages that began with, "*Didi* says that ..." But even these I had begun to believe were filtered.

Ah well ... as was my wont, I submitted to it all genially. My faith in Sudha and our relationship never wavered. But this little side trip to India was certainly teaching me a lot.

For one thing, there were no absolutes here. Her father, who, for all intents and purposes, hated my guts, would deign every evening to share a glass of whiskey with me while listening to old Mukesh songs. Her mother, who'd never spoken a word to me, would have my clothes laundered and ironed daily. Her numerous relatives would send various food items, sweetmeats and sundry gifts for me.

Sudhir, who'd offered his services as a tour guide, showed me the other side of India. The poverty and the wretchedness that co-existed in apparent harmony with opulence, extravagant wealth and waste.

A beggar-child would charm a rupee off you with a cheeky dance. A snake charmer would proffer his snake as a trophy. A rotund priest would stave off a skeletal shoeshine. Land of contrasts. Land of vagaries.

Our time in India was soon coming to an end and I seemed no closer to an answer. Sudha seemed so lost to me, that for the first time I wondered a bit fearfully if she herself had changed her mind.

An evening conference was called on the eve of our departure. There must have been twenty of them together in the room. Sudha looked small and scared. I yearned to take her in my arms - the world be damned!

But propriety did not permit. So, I just leaned awkwardly against the bookshelf, awaiting the verdict.

Sudha's dad cleared his throat and then addressed me.

"Adam, you are a nice boy and we like you. But you cannot marry Sudha. Sorry. You must go tomorrow. Sudha will not come with you." He shook his head sorrowfully.

I stood dumbfounded.

There was a lot of muttering till suddenly Sudha stood up. She walked towards me and held my hand.

"*Baba*, you have all had your say. I have listened patiently. Now please listen to me. This is the man I love. This is the man I will marry. He has shown me love, understanding and loyalty; he has been all that I've ever wanted in a life partner. I had hoped you would be able to see all of his fine qualities if I brought him here. I had hoped to get your blessings. However, if I don't, I will leave here without them. But leave I will."

"Sudha!" Her father's voice roared.

"Raj," an older, quieter voice from the corner interjected.

The old *Amma* said only a few lines. I understood none. There was pin-drop silence for a few moments and Sudha's dad tried responding, but a single word "*Bas!*" silenced him again. What had she said? I looked around in confusion at everyone. They seemed startled, as though confronted by an unpalatable truth. However impenetrable her words were, the import of them was not lost on me. She had silenced her son and quelled all opposition in one fell swoop. Unwittingly, in the last ten days, I had gained a powerful ally, and boy was I grateful! Before I could vocalise my gratitude, she expelled a loud fart. And none of us dared speak, or breathe. For *Amma* had spoken. From both ends.

Our big fat Indian wedding took place six months later. The tailor tut-tutted over my *sherwani*[5]. Sudha looked divine, even as she was weighed down by vast amounts of jewellery. The locality boys danced energetically led by a high-as-a-kite Sudhir. And *Amma* belched contentedly throughout.

❧

"Is that it?" you ask. Of course that's not all! Marriage isn't easy, let alone one that has differences in culture and height ... More especially, when you decide to relocate to a country that is alien in every way except that it has planted itself so securely in your heart that you have no choice. So you learn to get used to 'the stare' till it doesn't bother you anymore. You learn that "privacy" is a word that doesn't exist in this lexicon. You learn that when *Amma* speaks, you nod and smile, and hope to be spared her angry flatulence. You also learn of values: of love, of kindness, of respect, of largesse and of the tiny, tiny threads that weave you into a family so inextricably that even if you tried, you couldn't leave. Not that you'd ever try.

Sudha is losing patience with me.

"Adam, stop boring the poor child with that same old story! Oh, for the number of times you've told it! Everyone has a story. Ours isn't that special."

"Oh, but it is!" I chuckle, "It is to me."

Now, where's my *chai?*

3

KARMA-BAND

"Rashmi, can you hold her now? I have to get the passports out."

Rohit hands his four-year-old brat to me. She wriggles in protest, letting out a howl at my vice-like grip. I look towards Anita for help, but she refuses to meet my eye, taking out her Chanel compact to reapply her lip gloss instead .

The queue at New Delhi's Indira Gandhi International Airport isn't too long, but the guards at the entrance are taking forever, examining each passport against the tickets and studying every passenger's face suspiciously. There must be some kind of security alert, for I have never seen them being this diligent before. I hold on to the wriggling toddler, threatening and cajoling under my breath, still regretting the moment I'd agreed to this trip. Too late now, there is no turning back. A ten-day European tour seemed like the very break I'd needed, but now I can already envisage the nightmare it will be.

Rohit has handed our documents to the khaki-clad guard who is giving us all the once-over. Anita has sidled over to stand next to her husband. The guard indicates that she needs to remove her sunglasses. With an annoyed flick of her hair, she complies. Who except Anita would wear sunglasses at 2 in the morning? She still thinks she'll be mistaken for a film star after her faint brush with stardom ten odd years ago ("*They nearly cast me in the film darling!*"). There is no doubt that she turns heads, but more for her outlandish clothes and behaviour than for any star power she thinks she may possess.

Kat the brat is still wriggling and the guard looks at me and asks, "*Aapki hai*[1]?" I shake my head decisively and say, "No, she's their kid." He looks puzzled and I just shrug. Clearly, I will be the unpaid nanny on this trip, payback for the ticket and lodging I'm being offered gratis. And here I thought my brother had proffered me this holiday with altruistic intentions.

I finally settle the kid into her stroller once we're inside. Anita looks bored and not the slightest bit interested in the fruit of her womb. My brother looks distracted as he hunts for the counter to check-in at. This was meant to be a business trip for him, a solo one at that. Instead, thanks to Anita's multiple hissy fits, it's become a family holiday. No doubt the suggestion to take me along was hers too. Why pay for an *ayah*[2] when you can enlist your recently out-of-a-job, perennially single sister-in-law instead?

We march over to the Lufthansa counter. It's Business Class, no less. I perk up momentarily as I've only ever travelled Economy in my life. This will be nice. Then, Kat the brat decides to have a tantrum, and I miss out on all the lovely fawning by the airline staff, a privilege reserved for their more elite customers, things that I'll probably never get to experience again. I can see Anita preening under all the attention, the "Mr Shenoy, welcome back! Mrs Shenoy, please feel free to use our Business lounge before the flight." Never mind. The brat will have to sleep at some point. Then I intend to make the most of the flight and all its amenities.

Luckily, the queues at security aren't too bad either. Rohit has ensured, in his usual overly cautious manner, that we have arrived well ahead of time. Once again, Anita glides past, leaving the handling of the brat to me.

"Kat, baby, listen. *Bua*[3] has got some lovely storybooks in her bag. I promise to read them to you if you behave yourself, okay?"

"I want sweetieeeee!!" She wails, not impressed by my offer of edification.

Why am I surprised? No spawn of Anita's would be interested in books. It's sweets now, toys later, gadgets after that, and boys, makeup and clothes for the rest of her life. Like mother, like daughter.

No, stop! I really need to curb the sarcastic bitch within me. This is just a child, she can still be moulded. These ten days will be the perfect opportunity to try and un-brat the kid. After all, she is also Rohit's child and must have inherited some of his redeeming qualities?

After immigration, where the officer can't take his eyes off my sister-in-law's goopy lip gloss, we troop en masse towards Duty-Free. Anita apparently needs perfume, and not even Rohit's desperate appeal that perfume will be cheaper in Europe can deter her from her goal.

"Don't be so middle-class darling! I need perfume for the flight, and also for once we arrive. Didn't you say you have to rush straight to the office? You don't want me to meet your German colleague smelling of the aircraft, do you?"

Rohit lets her go. He stands next to me, looking spent. The brat is sucking on the lollipop that Anita pulled out of her capacious handbag and we have a few minutes of peace and quiet.

"You okay, bro?"

"Yeah, I'm fine. You?"

There was a time we could talk about anything, a time we were as close as siblings could be. But careers, success, failure, marriage, death and varying life paths have created an insurmountable distance between us, one that words, however heartfelt, cannot breach.

"I just wanted to say thank you for this trip."

He looks uncomfortable, as though caught out in the middle of a lie.

"No, don't worry about it. It's the least I could do ... after ... after ..."

"After my being made redundant?"

"That, and Sushma."

Sushma. I had wondered if he'd talk about her, or whether that was yet another fact to relegate to the background, like our middle-class upbringing that he regularly conceals behind his Armani suits and Harvard education. I know he's embarrassed by us, by our pedestrian lives, our simplicity, our inability to grasp how high he's climbed up the social and corporate ladder, and our underwhelmed response to it all. Even Sushma lies forgotten in the detritus of a past he has turned his back on. Which is why I am surprised he's mentioned her now. Has he been thinking about her?

I open my mouth to say something, then shut it again as I see Anita heading our way. She is laden with bags that contain more than just perfume. If there is one thing that Anita is good at, it's spending copious amounts of money.

"Baby, look what Mama bought you!"

She pulls out boxes of chocolates from the bags. This kid is going to be hyperactive on a sugar rush even before we board the aircraft! I do a mental eye-roll, hoping I'll be able to contain her.

Anita is still pulling stuff out. How could she have done so much damage to the credit card in such little time?

"I found a lovely Satya Paul tie for you Roh darling! It'll go so well with the suit you're wearing."

Rohit's face blanches as he sees the bright orange tie she is forcing upon him. No doubt it's fashion-forward and he'll be forced to wear it, forgoing the sensible navy one he has on now. Then she turns to me, with a saccharine-sweet smile. I wonder what horrors she has in store for me?

"Rash honey, I know you're not into designer stuff, so I bought you lipstick. You should really wear some makeup, you wouldn't look so old then."

She hands me a lurid pink lipstick that she knows I'll never ever wear. It'll be consigned to the heap of totally useless presents I have received from her in the last few years. It doesn't even hurt now, I am so used to her passive aggression towards me.

I wonder if we'll get a look-see at the Business lounge, but Anita has other ideas. And what Anita wants, Anita gets.

We start to amble towards the gate with a short halt at WHSmith. Anita wants to buy all the fashion magazines she can get her hands on and Rohit is looking for some business journal he's been reading about recently. While they wander, I keep a firm hold of the stroller, feeling quite smug that I've loaded up my Kindle with twenty new books. Whether I'll get to read them or not is an entirely different matter.

Kat keeps sticking her tongue out at people. She wants to show them how red it is thanks to the lollipop.

"Don't do that Kat, it's rude!"

"Why?"

"Because it is. Nice children don't stick their tongues out. It's rude and disrespectful."

She doesn't know what that means and clearly doesn't care. She is now digging her nose for treasure, producing the largest, greenest, most horrifying bit of snot to display to the world. I hurriedly clamp down on it with a tissue.

This is what happens if you leave the upbringing of your children to a steady rotation of *ayahs*. But who is to explain this to Anita, the bigger brat, born in the lap of luxury; spoiled and entitled beyond belief?

When Rohit decided to marry her, Ma and Pa had seen that as a sign that it was finally time to retire to Coorg. One meeting with Anita's folks had convinced them that oil and water would never mix. My father was an ex Government officer, habituated to a life filled with hard work, family values and an emphasis on good education. Anita's family couldn't have been farther apart from us if they tried. Business entrepreneurs, flashy and flamboyant, their lives were the stuff of glamour magazines. In a way, both sides had been confounded by their progeny's choice of spouse.

I was the only one who'd seen it coming.

When Sushma had been in her last stages of cancer, Rohit had been offered a plum job at SK Enterprises. Sushma had urged him to take it, still wanting that upward mobility for her brilliant husband, knowing full well that it would be a future denied to her. It was there that he'd met Anita, the boss' daughter, who'd taken an immediate shine to the quiet, self-effacing, handsome young man with a dying wife at home. She'd swooped in, playing Mother Teresa to a rapidly fading Sushma, plying her with gifts and flowers, forcing upon her attention she did not want, displaying her caring credentials to Rohit's incredulous family. Like a vulture she'd waited for the inevitable, waited to pick at the carcass of his grief, knowing exactly how to ensnare him in the process.

Ma and Pa had loved Sushma, my beautiful, quirky best friend who had become my sister-in-law. They had loved her like a daughter and mourned her for months after her death. They had been too grief-stricken to see what was happening right under their noses. I had tried warning Rohit, but by then he was already under Anita's spell. So, I too had watched helplessly from the sidelines as she, bit by bit, carted my brother away from us and established him in her ivory tower.

Five years and one child later, Rohit is a person I barely know. Would Sushma recognise him today? Would she still love him?

I hastily wipe away the tear that's rolled down my cheek. I'm not prone to bouts of sentimentality, but after Sushma's death, the seismic shift in my life left me little time to mourn her. Perhaps being in such close proximity to Rohit has brought it all back.

I feel a tug at my hand. Sticky little fingers insisting on attention. Kat is offering me her chocolate.

"*Bua*, for your boo-boo."

I kneel down and give her a hug. She's not a bad kid really.

"Miss Katrina Shenoy, what will your meal choice be?"

The air-hostess is a rather severe-looking German lady who looks at my niece in a disapproving manner. Kat ignores her, focussed on the shenanigans of the red-haired cartoon character on the screen in front of her.

"She'll take the pasta, and I'll have the chicken please."

The smile she bestows upon me is unexpected and lights up her entire face. She leans towards me and says, "You look like that actress ... that Indian one from 'The Life Of Pi'. Do you know her?"

Ah, Tabu! I have been compared to her before and find it incredibly flattering, although not quite believable. I smile and mouth my thank-you, hoping Anita hasn't heard the compliment or she'll be foaming at the mouth. Luckily for me, she hasn't. She's too busy knocking back the champagne and leafing through the latest edition of *Vogue*.

Rohit is buried deep in his papers, preparing for tomorrow morning's meeting. A meeting that was brought forward because his German counterpart has to rush off somewhere else straight after. This has given Rohit very little time to prepare, and with Anita interrupting him every two minutes with comments about some new handbag she's spied within the hallowed pages of her magazine, it'll be a wonder if he gets any work done at all.

Kat is watching her Disney movie, absolutely fixated by the plot. For the first time this evening, I feel relaxed. The seats are plush, they turn into beds with a flick of a switch. The pillow and blanket are so luxurious that I feel like snuggling into them and falling asleep straight away, except that I'll miss everything else if I do. I've already examined the contents of my amenity kit, which I will keep as a souvenir, unlike Anita who pulled everything out and chucked the bag to one side. The disposable slippers have been tucked into my handbag. I can hear Anita's voice in my head saying, "How middle-class, darling!" - but I don't care!

Our cabin doesn't seem very busy. There are a few people dotted around, some businessmen who look similarly occupied with work and some couples who are munching on the almonds and sipping on their drinks, watching their movies on their lovely large personal video screens. I'm too excited to watch anything. I want to take it all in and enjoy it. This is how the other half lives!

There is an American lady sitting behind me with a little girl around the same age as Kat next to her. The child has clung to her like a limpet from the time we boarded. I heard her explaining to the air hostess that she recently adopted her from an orphanage in India, and the entire process has been quite traumatic for the four-year-old who hadn't known home or family before. Now, she's petrified of all the changes and holding on for dear life to a stranger she's been told to call 'mother'.

I'd seen Anita shoot her a filthy look as they'd boarded behind us. Probably wondering why this hippie-looking middle-aged American and her adopted kid were seated right behind us, in Business class no less. In Anita's mind, anyone who doesn't conform to her version of glossy perfection is a sub-standard human, worthy only of disdain. I often wonder how Rohit tolerates her, but then realise belatedly that Rohit himself has morphed into a version of that glossy perfection.

The child behind me is still whimpering as the food arrives. Here I am trying to coax Kat to eat and behind me, the poor American woman is trying to disentangle the little girl from herself to try and feed her. We are both equally unsuccessful as Kat barely pays me any attention while I attempt to cajole her into eating a little bit of her prawn appetiser. She's too full on sweets and too absorbed in her movie to be interested. The little girl behind me, I gather her name is Radha, seems thin to the point of malnourishment, but this exotic food doesn't seem to be whetting her appetite either.

Rohit glances over at me from across the aisle. His forehead is creased as he sees me attempting to feed his daughter while his wife is tucking into her own meal with relish. I glimpse a spark of annoyance which disappears just as quickly as it appeared. Oh, you're in there somewhere brother, I just know it!

Between eating my own meal and feeding Kat, I manage somehow to drink a glass and a half of the excellent *Tempranillo* as well. The air hostess wants to top my glass up, but I stop her. I need to stay in my senses to take care of Kat, seeing as the mother has passed out cold after polishing off a bottle of champagne. Rohit indicates that he can take over from me, but I wave him off. Kat has fallen asleep with her headphones still on and her dinner barely eaten. I tuck her in gently, converting the seat into a bed and ensuring I've taken her headphones off. Then I sit back to enjoy the rest of my meal in peace.

❧

I'M WOKEN by a shrill cry that pierces through the quiet of the cabin. I sit up startled. How long have I been dozing? I look at Kat who is fast asleep, her little chest moving up and down in a steady rhythm. I glance over at Rohit and Anita who haven't woken either. Was I dreaming?

Then I hear a sob again. It's the child, the little girl behind me. I turn around to see that she's sitting bolt upright in her bed, looking absolutely terrified. Her mother is nowhere to be seen. I clamber out of my seat and go towards the child who cowers as I approach her.

"Shhhh, it's okay," I reassure her in a whisper. I sit at the foot of her bed, talking to her in a gentle undertone, not knowing or caring what I'm saying, just hoping that I can calm the poor child down.

"What are you doing?"

The American lady looks down at me suspiciously.

I stand up quickly and explain the situation. She looks shamefaced immediately.

"I was desperate to use the lavatory. I thought she'd be okay, she'd just fallen asleep. I'm so sorry you were disturbed."

"No, please don't worry about it. I couldn't help but overhear your earlier conversation with the air hostess. I think it's a wonderful thing you're doing, giving this child a home."

"Oh, I hope so. Her brothers and sisters can't wait to meet her."

She smiles at me as she cuddles a calmer Radha to her.

"You have other children?"

We are talking in whispers now. She's invited me to sit with her as she settles into her own seat, with Radha firmly ensconced in her lap.

"Yes, all adopted. Radha will make five."

"Wow!" I'm lost for words.

"It was a decision I made many years ago. Luckily, Jason, my husband, also agreed. Why bring more children into this world when there are so many that need a loving home?"

I feel strangely overwhelmed. I look at her and smile, hoping that my expression conveys all that I cannot put into words. She smiles back.

"Your little girl is really cute too."

"Kat is my niece. That's my brother and his wife right there. I'm just tagging along on this trip."

She looks at them and then looks at me, her eyebrows raised.

"Oh, you could have fooled me! Anyway, she's very sweet and you look very tired. Why don't we try and get some sleep now?"

I nod in agreement and return to my own seat, my thoughts all a jumble. Climbing over Kat, I settle myself into the bed, pulling the blanket over me and fall into a deep, dreamless slumber right away.

IT SEEMS like five minutes since I shut my eyes when I can hear Kat saying, "*Bua, susu*[4]!" It's bright daylight already and Kat is shaking me, indicating she needs to use the toilet.

I groan slightly as I sit up, my mouth feeling furry, a slight headache forming at my temples.

"Okay, *chalo*[5]." I take Kat to the toilet, looking over to see if my brother and his wife have stirred yet or not. Rohit isn't in his seat, but Anita is still asleep, her eye mask askew, slight snores escaping her open mouth. Thank goodness I don't need to wake up next to that every morning.

On our way to the toilet, I run into Rohit, who has freshened up for his meeting. The orange tie is on, giving him a slightly off-kilter look. I glance at it and then him, and he shrugs. He kneels down in front of Kat and asks, "Slept okay baby?"

She ignores him, pulling at my hand.

"*Susu!*"

I smile apologetically at him and let her lead me into the nearest toilet.

When we return, the breakfast service has started. I smile at the American lady, is it Susan? I can't remember her name although she did tell me at some point in our conversation last night. She smiles back at me, nodding at a peacefully asleep Radha who is curled up into a little ball, thumb in her mouth. I tilt my head towards Kat who is marching ahead of me, her ponytail droopy, but her attitude much in place. We grin as we recognise how different the girls are, despite being so similar in age.

Anita is waking up slowly, and when Kat tries to talk to her, she shoos her off.

"Not now baby! Mama is just getting up." She uncurls herself like a cat, yawning and stretching. She catches me staring and snaps, "What are you looking at?"

I glance away hurriedly. Maybe my disgust for her is only compounded by my memories of how lovely and unaffected Sushma was. There was never any artifice there, not a smidgen of selfishness either. How could Rohit have gone from that to this?

When breakfast arrives, Kat once again plants a mutinous scowl on her face. Neither the Bircher muesli nor the fruit proves tempting to her. She nibbles on the croissant and sips on the orange juice, then ignores the rest, concentrating on finishing her movie instead.

I eat my breakfast, opening up my Kindle to start reading a book that had been on my wish list for over a year. I've only just started when I hear Anita say "No!" really loudly. Rohit and she seem to be having some kind of a muted argument. He looks increasingly annoyed while she is getting even more belligerent. People are starting to look at them, and even the crew has shot a few concerned glances their way.

I get up quickly and go stand next to them.

"Guys, keep it down! People are staring. What's the matter? Can I help?"

"Rohit wants us to take a cab straight to the hotel while he goes for his breakfast meeting." She looks close to tears as she mouths this.

"So what's wrong with that? He'll join us later, won't he?"

"But I want to go for breakfast with him! I don't want to eat this crappy plane food. I want a proper breakfast!"

"Anita, you're just being unreasonable. It's a working breakfast, and will most likely be a continental one. Why would you want to bore yourself by coming there?" Rohit is trying to reason with a woman who has never been rational in her entire life.

"Why shouldn't I meet this Andrea woman as well? After all, I'm part owner of the company, I should have a say too."

"Do you even know what this meeting is about?"

"I don't care what it's about, I want to be there!"

"Fine! Be there then. Don't complain later that it was boring and that I didn't pay you any attention, as you did in New York."

Rohit looks at me, exasperation written all over his face.

"Rashmi, you and Kat head to the hotel. There are two rooms under my name. Take the one with the twin beds. At least you can get some rest this way."

"Oh no! I want Kat to come too." Anita looks at Rohit as if challenging him to a duel.

"Why would a four-year-old need to come to a meeting, Anita? What on earth are you thinking?"

She has set her jaw in a determined manner and I know that Rohit is going to lose this battle too.

"Why don't you want us to come? Don't want this Andrea to know you're a family man? Is that why you don't wear your wedding ring either?"

"Don't start with that nonsense again Anita! You know I don't wear jewellery of any kind. And why does Andrea need to know anything about my private life? This is work. I like to keep the two separate."

As they continue to argue and bicker, I make my way back to my seat. Jealousy is such an ugly emotion and if Anita knew my brother at all she'd know that infidelity does not exist in his lexicon. But of course, she'd assign the worst motives to him, because her own intentions were suspect from the very start. Isn't it funny how we see our own animus mirrored in others?

❧

When we finally arrive in Frankfurt, we have to wait on the jet bridge for our strollers. The American lady waits alongside us. I can see Kat sizing up Radha. Then she reaches inside her little backpack, pulls out a lollipop and offers it to her. Radha shrinks back, hiding behind Susan.

"It's okay honey. The nice girl is giving you her lollipop."

Encouraged thus, Radha emerges shyly from behind her adoptive mother and takes the proffered lollipop. In no time at all the two girls are friends, pulling at each other's hair and giggling together. Susan and I start chatting about how long their flight to Seattle will be and how different Radha is likely to find her new home.

Suddenly I hear Anita pronounce loudly, "Oh God, the smell!"

She's looking at Radha as she says this and I move quickly to block her from view before Susan figures that her child is being criticised. I have a sneaky suspicion that Susan is quite capable of turning into Mother bear if required. I distract her by talking about the job I've just lost.

"Last in, first out. I mean, I really loved the job, but what can one do? They were trimming the fat and I was one of the casualties."

"That must have been tough! Are you looking for something else?"

"Not yet. I'm just licking my wounds right now, I guess." I laugh as I say this, realising that I've probably overdone the metaphors. She laughs back, then looks at me appraisingly before rummaging in her bag.

"Here, take my card. I might have something interesting for you."

"But aren't you based out of the US?"

"We have a branch in New Delhi too."

Before I can look at the card or say anymore, the strollers arrive.

With a quick wave, Susan deposits Radha in her stroller and heads off towards the connecting gates. Kat immediately has a meltdown.

"Friend!!! I want friend ...!"

"Oh stop it, Kat! Why were you playing with that smelly child anyway? Disgusting! She looked like a guttersnipe."

With that pronouncement, she sweeps away, leaving me to negotiate her cranky child into the stroller. Rohit, as usual, has missed the entire episode, too busy talking business over the phone.

We walk at varying paces. Kat has settled down after being handed an iPad to watch more cartoons on. Desperate times require desperate measures, even though I'm not in favour of young children being hooked on gadgets. Rohit is looking increasingly harried as the time for his meeting approaches.

Anita is the only one who looks calm. She has changed into an all-cream ensemble, with a Louis Vuitton shawl slung over one arm and beautiful pewter suede heels on her feet. Her blonde highlights are artfully tousled and the sunglasses are back on. The lip gloss has been applied several times over, leaving her mouth looking like an oil slick. She is reeking of the Christian Dior perfume she bought at Duty-Free. I try to walk as far behind her as possible so that I'm not caught downwind in her draught.

We pile into a taxi together. I get a whiff of something foul and ignore it at first. The smell comes and goes and I wonder if it's the taxi driver, but Rohit, who is sitting next to him doesn't seem to have noticed. Anita, who is drenched in Dior and putting on another layer of lip gloss probably has no sense of smell left. I look at Kat and ask her quietly, "Did Kat do a *put-put*?" It's baby talk for a fart. Kat completely ignores me, fiercely concentrating on her iPad. I figure it must have been her, and roll down the window slightly to let the smell escape.

I examine the card that Susan handed to me at the airport. She's only the CEO of one of the largest conglomerates in the world! To think that I may have a chance, even a tiny one, to gain a foothold there, sends my mind spinning.

"Rohit?" I look at the back of his head. He turns slightly towards me. "That was Susan Miller, sitting behind us."

"The woman you were talking to? The one with the kid?"

"Yes. She's given me her card. Says she might have something for me, by way of a job."

He twists his body, turning to look at me straight in the face.

"Rashmi, what bloody, brilliant luck! You do realise that this could be the making of you? Send her an email as soon as possible, before she forgets who you are!" He grins at me, genuinely pleased.

"Who, that woman with the smelly child? Why would you email her? Did you see how she was dressed? They must've upgraded her! How else could they afford to sit in Business class? I tell you, the types of people that are travelling these days ..."

Anita carries on with her rant. I tune her out, but not before exchanging a glance with Rohit that is loaded with meaning. Has he finally begun to see what he married?

Twenty minutes later we arrive at the offices of Hofmann & Co. We tumble out of the taxi with Rohit trying to handle the luggage and pay the taxi driver. I try to help, but handling Kat and the luggage is not easy and I can see how this whole endeavour is so frustrating for Rohit. Anita just stands to one side, completely removed from us, as though a queen bee to her minions.

An astonished doorman lets us in while calling out in German to another associate who runs up to us to help us with the luggage. Then, once Rohit establishes who exactly he is here to meet, we are ushered up in the lift to the fifth floor.

I look around at the state-of-the-art office interior in awe. It's an absolutely stunning structure made of steel and glass, with a futuristic vibe and minimalist interiors. The thick white carpets absorb all the noise and aside from the faint hum of the elevators, there is almost pin-drop silence in the waiting room we've been escorted to.

Anita takes herself off to the restroom after enquiring loudly and obnoxiously of its whereabouts. I sip on the *Illy* coffee I've been offered while Rohit peruses his file once more. Again I get a whiff of something noxious. I check under my shoes to see if I've stepped on something, but they're clean. I know that Kat is potty trained, and I did take her in the morning, so it can't be her. What if it's Rohit?

"Hey, Rohit ..."

He looks up at me with a frown.

"Can you smell something funny?"

"What?"

"A funny smell, like, really bad. It's been following us around ..."

He sniffs the air and picks up on it too.

"Yes, I can smell it ... Is it her?"

I take Kat out of her stroller even as she protests, and try and sniff her bum.

"No, I don't think so."

"What could it be?"

Even as we are trying to establish the source, in comes a tall, willowy blonde.

"Hello, Rohit! Nice to see you again." She shakes his hand and then plants a kiss on each cheek. "This must be your lovely wife."

"Uh, actually that's my sister, and that's my little girl, Kat. Rashmi, this is Andrea Hofmann."

We shake hands and I immediately understand why Anita was so insecure. This woman is not just stunningly beautiful, she is also probably far more educated and accomplished than Anita could ever be. I stand back as they fall into their business discussion straight away. I can see that she is a bit mystified by our presence but too polite to address it.

She's just put her hand on Rohit's back to lead him into the conference room when Anita enters the room.

"Hi!" She plants herself in front of them. "I'm Rohit's wife and Mr Sukhija's daughter."

Andrea looks nonplussed but regains her composure quickly.

"Welcome to Germany. I understand you will be going on a family holiday after this?"

"That's the plan." Anita is openly hostile and I can see Rohit trying to ward off the next salvo by declaring, "Anita really wanted to sit in on the meeting, if that's okay by you Andrea?"

"Well, why not?" She looks at me and asks, "Will you both be alright here?"

The smell has been getting stronger and I can tell that Andrea is trying not to sniff too hard. She probably thinks one of us has let go.

"What is that smell?" Anita, ever the diplomat, says what everyone else is thinking. She marches over to Kat and sniffs at her. "Baby, have you done potty?"

Kat looks up, frightened by her mother's unexpected interest in her. She shakes her head, starting to sniffle as she does.

Anita yanks her out of the stroller and much to everyone's horror pulls down her pants. They are clean, but by now Kat is starting to hiccup in fear.

"Open your mouth!" Anita commands, but Kat tries to pull away from her.

"Anita really ..."

"Please Mrs Shenoy ..."

"You're frightening her ..."

All of us try to intervene, but Anita pays us no heed. She's shaking Kat now. "What have you got in your mouth? Open! NOW."

Quite suddenly, perhaps out of fear or perhaps unable to hold it all in any longer, Kat vomits out the contents of her mouth all over Anita's suede shoes. Bits of Bircher muesli and last night's prawns stick to the shoes and the carpet, sending up an unimaginable stink.

I look at the debris in disbelief. The child had been storing all that food, hamster-like in her mouth for the duration of the flight. Before any of us can say anything, Anita slaps Kat across the face with such fury that she nearly goes flying.

"Enough!" Rohit stands above her, shielding Kat behind him. "Get out! Go to the hotel right now and sort yourself out. We'll talk about this once I'm finished here."

"It's *her* fault!" Anita looks at me in fury. "She should have known. She was supposed to be taking care of her."

"Stop it, Anita! We are her parents, we should have been taking care of her."

Andrea steps in.

"Mrs Shenoy, I will arrange a car to take you back to the hotel. I think that perhaps everybody needs a rest after that long flight, hmm?" She tries placing a hand on Anita's shoulder to calm her down.

"Get your hands off me, you blonde bitch! I know what you're about. You can't wait to have my husband to yourself, right? That's why this meeting was set up in a hurry! You think I don't know?"

Andrea steps back and gives Anita a cold, assessing look, a look that would make anyone shrivel. Her voice is icy as she says, "Rohit, I will be waiting in the conference room. My flight is at 1 pm. If you're not there in the next fifteen minutes, I will consider this meeting cancelled."

After she leaves, I go over to Kat who is still trembling and hiding behind Rohit. She clings to me as I take her to one side. I don't want her to witness this scene between her parents, but don't know where else to go. I take the picture books I'd brought for her and start reading from them. She climbs onto my lap, still smelling slightly foul, but calming down slowly, imperceptibly.

THE ARGUMENT between Rohit and Anita is a short one. The divorce will be long and painful in comparison. These two were never meant to be together, they were always as different as chalk and cheese. Hijacking a vulnerable man, a grieving husband at that, no matter what motivation there may be, is bad karma. However, turning your back on your family and who you really are, regardless of the circumstances, is equally bad karma.

Perhaps Anita, who was spoiled, petted and indulged from the start, expected that life owed her every single thing she ever set her eyes on and coveted. Perhaps it never crossed her mind that money couldn't buy it all, especially not integrity or respect. Perhaps she never realised that that old adage was as true as the day it was written - you only reap what you sow.

As for Rohit, there had been time enough for him to see the error of his ways, time enough to bow out before a child entered the scene, time enough to figure out that love cannot be replaced by money or stature. Five painful years did not have to culminate in a scene that only lasted five painful minutes at best.

So, yes, the divorce will be long and painful. Kat will suffer the most, but Rohit, Anita and the rest of us will suffer too. Sometimes, the suffering of the innocent is the worst karma of all. As adults, we have choices that we make, paths that we take - willingly, wilfully, with our eyes open to the consequences. These paths are determined by our natures, by our motivations and by the intent behind the motivation. If the intent is corrupt, nothing good can emerge from it. Rohit and Anita will have years to reap the harvest of the fracture of their family. As a bystander and a relative, at once involved and separated, I can only hope to provide a safe harbour to their child. The suffering of the innocent is the worst karma of all.

Hopefully though, at the end of it, we will be free to live our lives in whichever fashion we choose. Aside from Kat, nothing else will bind us to Anita, her family, their wealth or their social standing. Freedom can never be overrated, just as karma can never be underrated.

At age thirty, it is a lesson I've imbibed from my parents and from life. I see the paths, the choices that lie ahead of me. I see who I'd rather be: a Susan rather than an Anita. Inner worth trumps outer lustre any day. Our values lead us to lives that are fulfilled by more than just material possessions. Our values lead us to our karma.

Because here's the thing: karma is an elasticised judge. Like a rubber-band that, when stretched beyond capacity invariably rebounds on you, so does she. And when she does, there is nowhere to duck, nowhere to hide and nowhere to run.

A lesson we would all do well to learn.

4

THE BEST LAID PLANS

When Hiten fell down and broke his clavicle, he had no idea it would change his life. Up until then, he had been a reclusive retiree, happy to spend his days listening to old K.L. Saigal songs, and drinking his sole glass of whiskey every evening. Thirty years of being divorced had left him morose, unfriendly and unapproachable. He did not like women, children or animals, they were anathema to him. He did like music, but only really old music that no one listened to anymore, especially because it made him feel separate from the masses who bopped to whatever nonsense was paraded as music these days. And he loved books. At sixty-five, he'd decided that if the rest of his days were to be spent in the company of these two loves, then he would be very content indeed.

Life, of course, had other plans.

Living in the duplex apartment left to him by his elderly parents, Hiten had never worried about going up and down the stairs, frequently sprinting up to fetch the sundry items his old mother would forget in her bedroom. After her death, he still sprinted from force of habit, till time and age started slowing him down. Now he was content to take the stairs at a more sedate pace, happy that unlike a lot of his peers, he didn't find himself winded each time he climbed up the dozen steps to the next floor. So, the accident was something he could never have foreseen happening to him.

His foot slipped as he was going downstairs, carrying his tray with the remnants of his weekend breakfast and coffee. The newspaper had been balanced on the side of the tray, obscuring his view. Had his hands been free, he might have been able to break his fall. As it was, he landed awkwardly, the tray flying out of his hands, his body hitting the concrete floor of his living room, his shoulder slamming into the ground, his cry of shock and pain bouncing off the walls of the empty house.

He lay there for a while, his body twisted at an unnatural angle. The first thought that crossed his mind was that Maya had not swept under the sofa as he had instructed her to, the dust being thick; months-old layers of it sitting there undisturbed. His second thought was that if he had died, no one would have found him till Maya came by on Monday, her erratic schedule accommodating the retired 'uncle' at the very end of her cleaning rounds. After having lain there for a while, strange thoughts crossing his mind, he tried moving his feet, slowly inching his body into a comfortable position. Each tiny movement sent a fresh wave of pain up his arm, leaving him in no doubt that something was broken.

Whom could he call on a Sunday? The neighbours he never spoke to, his ex-colleagues were just that, he had no friends, and Miriam, his mother's old nurse had returned to Kerala. She had left him a number just in case, but could she really help from all the way in Kerala?

Nevertheless, he shuffled towards the phone, using his good hand to retrieve the phone book and look for her number.

She answered after a few short rings, sounding perplexed to be hearing from him after four years.

"Mr Patel?" Her T's and L's still rolled with a heavy Malayali accent.

"Yes Miriam, it is Hiten Patel. You nursed my mother, remember? Before she died?"

"Yes sir, I remember. She was a very nice lady." The 'lady' came out as 'layddee', and immediately brought back memories of Miriam's soothing voice and plump person, caring for his mother in her last days.

"Is everything wokay Mr Patel?"

He realised he'd been silent for a beat too long.

"Yes, well ... no, actually. I think I might have broken my shoulder. I just fell down the stairs."

"Ohhh! That is no good, sir. You should be going to the hospital right away, not to be calling me ..."

Of course, that would have made the most sense. What could Miriam possibly do for him in Ahmedabad, while she was in Kerala? But his instinctive need to hear her voice must have been connected to the comfort he associated her with. Comfort she'd provided to his mother in her dying days, comfort he craved for himself now.

"Hello? Hello?"

"Yes, I'm here, Miriam." He answered wearily, realising the futility of the call. "I'm sorry, I don't know what made me dial your number. I guess I'll call a taxi instead."

"No, please wait Mr Patel. I will call my nephew who lives there. He will take you to hospital."

"That's really not necessary Miriam, but thank you. I will manage."

He was fully prepared to end the call and make his own way, the shock having receded and pragmatism taken its place. But he hadn't reckoned for Miriam's tenacity. After five minutes of wrangling, he finally resigned himself to being driven by Miriam's nephew to the nearest hospital. She insisted and in his pain and loneliness, he had neither the heart nor the strength to argue with her.

Wincing with every move, he dressed himself slowly, haltingly. Never having taken a sick-day off in his entire career, he now wondered how he would fill his days, his right arm being out of commission for the foreseeable future. Loneliness did not bother him, but debility did. His soul craved solitude and independence, yet his condition would allow for neither.

The doorbell rang a short while later, when Hiten was still in the process of tucking his shirt into his trousers. The young man who stood at the door looked uncannily like Miriam - a younger, more masculine version, but the family resemblance was unmistakable. He sported a large handlebar moustache on his upper lip and whilst his smile was very white and very broad, his eyes signalled concern.

"Mr Patel? My auntie told me to fetch you." His English was better than Miriam's but the Malayali accent lingered, and Hiten felt an immediate unexpected feeling of relief, as though Miriam had reached across miles and several states and patted his head soothingly.

He barely spoke to the young man sitting beside him in the car, who'd provided a name which Hiten had forgotten straight away. He only thought of him as Miriam's nephew. But his thoughts were a jumble of pain, nostalgia and fear. He wasn't sure which hospital to go to, so the nephew had decided for him. As they drove there, Hiten cradled his right arm with his left, realising for the first time in his life how alone he really was.

Sapna had been the fifth match proposed for him. His parents had liked the fact that she was an accountant, they had assumed that since he was a practical, pragmatic man, neither showing nor needing affection, a girl who excelled at numbers would perhaps suit him equally in temperament. How wrong they had been! His sister had tried warning them, saying that maybe Hiten was better off single, that he was happy as he was, but as parents they wanted to see both their children settled into wedlock. He had never voiced an opinion; he had none to voice. As far as he was concerned, marriage was a necessary evil, a partnership that had served people like his parents and his sister well. He could see the advantages of it and so, hadn't protested when Sapna was the girl his parents decided upon.

Right from the start it was a disaster. Sapna was needy and demanding, wanting something from him that he could not comprehend or provide. Their rows had gotten louder and more vicious. He took to spending longer hours at work, hoping his absence would help her settle into the household with his parents, avoiding her accusing eyes and his parents' helpless attempts to mollify and cajole.

Two years of what he mentally began to define as 'living hell' finally came to an end when she filed for divorce. His parents, beaten and abashed by the failure of his marriage, never once asked him to remarry. Perhaps his sister's moving away to Australia was the deciding factor in their wanting to keep their one and only son close to them, under their roof. Perhaps they finally realised that Hiten would never really need a life companion the way other people did. At any rate, it was an arrangement that suited them all.

Now, as he watched the traffic passing them by on the other side of the road, he wondered if there had been something wrong with him all along? Why wasn't he like other people, requiring love or companionship? Why did the absence of another human being in his life not bother him as much as it should have? Yes, he missed his parents. He had wept privately at his father's untimely demise, but had been secretly relieved at his mother's release from suffering. Yes, he sometimes longed to see his sister and her family with the multiple grandchildren, more often than their sporadic visits, but not enough for him to make the journey to Melbourne himself.

Is that why, isolated and alone, he was now at the mercy of strangers?

THE NEPHEW PULLED up in front of the Civic Hospital, not one that Hiten would have chosen had he been thinking straight. But he got out of the car slowly, looking around him. People were milling about, looking at him curiously as they walked by. Some young men loitered near the door, and sari-clad women pushed past with a sense of urgency. This was a hospital that catered to the normal *janta*[1]. He could have afforded to go somewhere better, but how was the nephew to know that?

"Please, Mr Patel, you go inside. I will park car and come."

So Hiten walked in, observing the hustle and bustle with a vague sense of disbelief. When was the last time he'd visited a Government hospital? Perhaps when their servant boy had taken ill with severe diarrhoea and Hiten's parents had insisted on him being taken there. He'd forgotten the grime, the noise, the crowds and the sheer helplessness written on the faces of family members who waited to hear news of their loved ones. What on earth was he doing here?

"Mr Patel, Mr Patel ..." The nephew had obviously managed to find parking fairly quickly as he was now being led towards the receptionist, a bored middle-aged woman, who glanced at him with barely-disguised irritation.

The nephew explained the situation, and now Mr Patel found himself being led down another corridor, to wait outside the doctor's office. He felt dizzy and slightly sick at this point and had to lean on the nephew for support.

"W ... what is your name?"

"Thomas, Mr Patel." He didn't sound annoyed as he patiently lowered him into a chair and stood by him like a sentry.

"Thomas, you seem to know this hospital well?"

"Yes, sir. My wife going to have our baby here."

"Your wife?"

"Yes sir. She is nurse here, but she also going to have our baby. I will call her now."

"No, no, there is no need ..." Hiten shook his head, not wanting to meet yet another stranger in this already painful day.

The doctor was calm and professional, much to Hiten's surprise. He confirmed that it was a fractured clavicle and not a dislocated shoulder, after an X-ray. He then fashioned him a sling and advised painkillers and bed rest for a while.

"Do you have anyone to take care of you?"

"No."

"Do you live alone?"

"Yes."

"Do you have a maid?"

"Only a cleaner."

"What about food?"

"I cook for myself."

"Mr Patel," the doctor seemed exasperated by the succinct

answers he'd been receiving, "you really need to find some kind of temporary help. Clearly, you will not be able to manage on your own. So, I'd advise you to hire someone in the meantime."

"You!" The doctor glanced at Thomas. "Can you arrange somebody?"

"Me?" Thomas looked confused, but then beamed down at the doctor as though struck by sudden inspiration. "I will ask someone sir. We will find solution."

As they came out of the room, Hiten once again leaning on Thomas for support, he saw a short, plump girl in a nurse's uniform, with frizzy hair pulled back in a bun, waiting outside. She rushed towards them full of smiles and apologies.

"This is Lola, my wife." Thomas introduced his pregnant wife proudly.

Hiten managed a weak smile before sliding down to the floor, the world suddenly going dark on him.

He found himself waking up in a hospital bed when everything outside was dark. How long had he been out? His throat felt dry and he felt the first rumblings of hunger. His entire right arm throbbed, from collar to wrist. He'd obviously been put in a separate room, instead of in a ward. He looked around him for some sign of life, but the room was dark and silent with just a faint light from a distance penetrating the gloom. Swinging his legs off the bed, he tried standing up, but another dizzy spell had him falling back upon the bed.

"Oh please, don't stand up!" Lola came rushing at him from nowhere. "I had just gone to organise some dinner for you."

She had a slightly squeaky, childish voice that sounded breathless, as though all she ever did was rush around, which he supposed as a nurse, she probably did.

She held a little packet in her hand, and he could smell the food in it. His stomach growled in response.

"It is only some *rotli dal*[2] but it is homemade."

He tucked into it with relish. He had been subsisting on toast and cheese ever since the last cook had quit. This was delicious.

She sat on a chair next to his bed, watching him approvingly.

"Where am I?" He looked at the vast, mostly empty room that was lit by a single lightbulb that Lola had switched on.

"This is the new wing of the hospital that the Government gave us money for. This is where the new Maternity Ward will be, once it's finished. Lots of equipment arriving in a few days, but until then, I thought you could stay here. If you give a small donation to the hospital, the administration will look the other way."

Hiten looked around the empty room dotted with a few beds here and there, and wondered whether to agree to this crazy deal. But what choice did he have? He could return home and try to manage on his own, but that would be foolhardy. He could try and go to a better hospital but that could prove very costly. Whereas here, there was medical aid at hand and also a bed and possibly food and company, for a nominal fee.

"I should pay Thomas and you as well." Hiten spoke aloud, voicing his last thought.

Lola stood up, brushed down her skirt, then smiled as she took the empty plate out of his hands.

"Auntie Miriam told us to take care of you and that is what we are doing. We do not need any payment for that."

THE NEXT FEW days fell into an odd sort of pattern. The construction workers would arrive at around 10am and the banging and drilling would begin, so Hiten knew that any peace and quiet was impossible for the rest of the day. After the hospital breakfast of toast and tea brought to him by a taciturn orderly, Hiten would take himself for a walk around the facilities.

Not a chatty person himself, he enjoyed watching rather than participating, and once his initial dismay at landing in such a chaotic environment had faded, he started to recognise the rhythms of life there as well.

The different shifts, the various doctors and nurses, the orderlies, the pharmacists, all became familiar to him in the week he was housed as a paying guest in the semi-finished wing of the hospital. He too, became a familiar figure, wandering amongst everyone, always alone, somewhat aloof, but not threatening, merely observing.

The best part of his day was when Lola brought him some home made fare. He'd grown to thoroughly enjoy her cooking and wondered - would offering her a job as his cook be a step too far? She would sit by his bedside, quietly knitting booties for her baby, waiting for him to finish, before checking his sling and administering his medication as prescribed by the doctor.

Somehow, together, they fell into a quiet companionship, neither expecting nor demanding conversation from each other. He would watch her head bent over her knitting needles, her brow furrowed in concentration, and wonder if, had he had a daughter, she would have been around the same age. Whether she would have looked after him with the same attentiveness and solicitude.

Thomas, on the other hand, was the chatty one who would turn up every evening after Lola had gone home, to share a sneaky drink with Hiten. It was a cheap rum procured from a local liquor store, but Hiten didn't have the heart to turn him down. After all, it was thanks to Thomas that he was here, albeit for a short while.

It was on Sunday, a week after his fall, that Thomas walked in looking crestfallen.

"Sir, they are moving the equipment in tomorrow."

"So I will have to move out?"

"Yes sir. I would ask you to come stay with us, but we only have one room and Lola sleeps on the single bed. In her condition, I don't want her to sleep on the floor ..."

"I understand." Hiten got up from the bed immediately. "I am better anyway, so it will be good to go home."

Thomas helped him pack up the few belongings he'd had him bring over, then helped him into his car.

"Will you ..." Hiten cleared his throat. "Will you and Lola visit me?"

"Visit? Sir, Lola is already at your house. She is cooking you dinner. I hope you don't mind?"

Hiten had forgotten that he had given Thomas his house keys to procure his clothes and other necessities. Had he forgotten to take them back, or had Thomas deliberately not returned them? He had no valuables in the house, but there was a little bit of cash under the mattress. Would Thomas have found it? He looked into his worried face and immediately regretted his thoughts. What made him so suspicious of people's motives, even when they were as kind and helpful as Thomas and Lola had been?

"No, no, I don't mind. It's very good of Lola to do this."

"Well, sir, Auntie Miriam was very worried about you. She told us to look after you, and Lola, well, she thinks you need to be fed a little better."

They walked out of the hospital together. A few of the nurses waved at them and he wondered if it was Thomas they were acknowledging or himself. He waved back self-consciously when he realised that they were bidding him goodbye.

In Thomas' car, he asked him about his job.

"Well sir, I am a chauffeur for the Desai family. They are very good to me and very understanding. Only thing is, I cannot take any sick leave. So, after Lola has baby, I need to go back to work."

"When is Lola due?"

"Oh, in twelve weeks sir."

"Will she carry on working till then?"

"No sir. She will stop at the end of this month. She is looking forward to it, I can tell you. Poor thing, her feet get so swollen from being on them all day long."

"Why is she not going back to Kerala to deliver the baby? Isn't that what most young women do, go back to their maternal home?"

"But where will she go sir? She is an orphan only."

At this, Hiten subsided into silence. He had run out of conversation, but Thomas carried on talking, not noticing. Hiten let his words wash over him.

An orphan. That's what he was as well. It was the first time he had articulated that thought within himself. So what if he was sixty five years old? He had still belonged to a family; been a son, a brother, and very briefly, a husband too. Now, he felt completely alone. His soul ached with a loneliness that he had hidden even from himself.

"... whenever that is, I will take you to the hospital."

Thomas glanced sideways at him, waiting for his response.

"I'm sorry, I didn't catch the last bit?"

"Your collar bone needs to be checked by the doctor in the next few days to see if it is healing well. I will take you, sir."

"Oh."

Hiten was perfectly capable of calling for a taxi, now that he had recovered from the initial shock and gotten used to his temporary debility, but the thought of Thomas coming to fetch him pleased him unaccountably.

As Thomas parked outside, Mrs Shah from two doors away walked up to him, her vegetable basket overflowing with her recent purchases.

"Are you okay Mr Patel? We saw strange people going in and out of the house and got quite worried. Oh! What happened to your arm?"

Suddenly Hiten felt exhausted. He didn't want to have to explain himself to the neighbourhood gossip, but felt that he needed to.

"Thank you for your concern, Mrs Shah. I had a fall and Thomas and his wife have been helping me out."

She gave a suspicious look to Thomas who was standing like a bodyguard by his side.

"You could have asked us ..."

"Yes, thank you. I ... I need to get inside."

Thomas held his good elbow, leading him indoors. Hiten knew that Mrs Shah was just nosing around for information. After his mother's death, he had cut himself off from the neighbourhood circle, one that his parents had been a happy part of. The very thought of having to mingle, chat about inanities, and show superficial concern had always filled him with horror. So he had retreated, preferring his own company to that of the larger world.

Inside, he was greeted by the most delicious smell of home cooking, an aroma that immediately brought back memories of happier times.

Lola came out of the kitchen, a rolling pin in hand.

"Oh Mr Patel! Welcome home. You are looking so much better. I have made some tea and *dhokla*[3] for you. Thomas, *aa chaaya vegam kondu vaa*[4]! I am just finishing off the *rotlis.*"

Hiten allowed Thomas to help him into the armchair. While Thomas and Lola bustled around him, he wondered once again if he could offer them both employment. Then he checked himself, knowing full well that he was incapable of giving them the salaries they required. However, he certainly intended to compensate them for their time and their efforts once the baby arrived. They could not possibly refuse a generous cash gift, if it were given as a blessing for the new baby.

He was still lost in thought when he heard the crash. Thomas jumped up from the chair he had just settled into for lunch, and rushed towards the kitchen. Hiten moved at a slower pace, no less alarmed when he heard Lola moaning.

"What is it? What's happened?"

The rolling pin had fallen on the floor, taking the *rotli dabba*[5] with it. Lola was clutching her stomach as another moan escaped her.

"Something is wrong Mr Patel ... I have to take Lola to the hospital ... the baby could be coming ... "

"But ... but she isn't due for another twelve weeks you said ..." Hiten was confused, but Thomas just ignored him, focusing on his wife, leading her out gently.

Hiten stood to one side, letting them pass.

"Wait! Thomas, here. Please take this money. It's not much, but it may help."

Thomas looked up at him and said, "That is very kind of you sir, but right now we need your prayers more than we need money."

Abashed, Hiten watched Thomas and Lola make their way to the car parked outside. He anxiously watched the car till it turned the corner, and then went back inside to clear up.

All evening he paced the floor, waiting for some news. He had tidied up as much as he could with only one hand in commission. He'd noticed that Lola had filled his refrigerator with enough food to last him a few days, but his appetite was lost to worry.

Were mother and baby okay? What did it mean for an infant to arrive this early? His knowledge of babies was limited to what he'd seen on television. He knew even less about pregnancy and labour, but he remembered his mother saying what a tough time she'd had while carrying him. It had taken her forty eight hours before he'd arrived, and she'd sworn off having babies after that.

If that's how long it took, maybe there was no point in worrying just yet? He would call Thomas' mobile in a day or two to find out. Then he poured himself a glass of whiskey and put on an old K. L. Saigal record on his HMV record player, and soothed himself back into his everyday life.

WHEN A FEW DAYS had gone by with no news, Hiten allowed the minor anxiety that he'd been harbouring to finally surface. He tried Thomas' number several times, but the phone was always switched off. All sorts of thoughts started to cross his mind. Could it all have been a con? Had they stolen all his valuables and absconded?

He went upstairs in a hurry and checked under the mattress. The Rs. 20,000 he kept there for emergencies was still intact. Then he looked inside his wardrobe, reaching into a jacket pocket, and took out his father's old Rolex watch. Finally, he felt around among his underclothes and found his mother's gold chain and his own wedding ring, still intact. He sat down on the bed, relief and shame coursing through him. They had taken nothing. Instead they had given him their time and their consideration and he had repaid that by mistrusting their motives.

He tried Thomas' number again, with the call going into voicemail once more. Then he rang Miriam. When she answered, he babbled out all his concerns and frustrations to her.

"Mr Patel, sir, please ..."

"... and I have been calling all day today, but Thomas is not answering his phone. What has happened? Why has he not informed me?"

Miriam waited for him to run out of steam, then patiently explained what had happened.

"Lola deliver baby yesterday, but she is tooo little only. Now baby in special unit and Lola very weak. Thomas taking care of them, that is only why his phone not on."

"Oh." Suddenly Hiten felt foolish and selfish, as if his own worries had been greater than everyone else's.

"Is she going to be okay?"

"Who sir? Lola or baby?"

"Both, I guess."

"I hope so sir. Baby is premature, so nothing is for sure."

The conversation tapered off and Hiten hung up after thanking Miriam, his mind still in turmoil. What could he do to help? How could he get in touch with the young parents? Could he provide them with financial assistance or maybe help out some other way?

Another day went by, with him deliberating the pros and cons of just turning up at the hospital. Maya came home and he finally had her sweep under the sofas, ignoring her mutinous scowls. His mind was still preoccupied.

Finally he decided on a course of action. He ordered a taxi to take him to the local market where he picked up flowers, a box of *penda*[6] and a decorative envelope to put Rs. 2001 in. His mother had told him years ago that giving money in round numbers was considered inauspicious, and to always add 1 rupee to the amount. From there he ordered the taxi to take him to the Civic hospital.

In the few days he'd been away, the hospital had carried on as always with the hum and throb of life it was accustomed to. Sick people went in, some came out cured, others succumbed and the circle of life carried on in births, deaths, disease, accidents and disasters.

He went up to the grumpy receptionist who looked up with a scowl and then beamed when she saw it was him.

"Mr Patel! So good to see you again sir. Are you here for your appointment with the doctor?"

"No, I wanted to enquire about Lola. Lola Mathews?"

"Lola? Oh, nurse Lola? Yes, yes. She is in the maternity ward but the poor baby is not well. Born too early you see. Chances are not good." She shook her head mournfully.

"Can I see her? Lola, I mean. Is she receiving visitors?"

"Visitors? Only Thomas comes to see her. The nurses drop by because they are her friends, but no one else has been. Of course, you can go in during visiting hours, but that is not till 4 pm."

He glanced at his watch. It was only 2:30 pm.

"I'll wait."

"Okay." She smiled at him and went back to her work.

He wandered over to the chairs set aside for people such as him. The flowers had wilted a bit in the heat, but he set them on the chair next to him along with the box of *penda* and resumed his observation of the people around him.

All life is to be found in busy places such as hospitals and railway platforms. Here, no one stopped to reflect. They were too busy rushing hither thither, whether that was to another destination or in search of treatment, a balm, a cure.

Over there was a mother cradling her toddler who clung apathetically to her, burning up with fever; here was a son helping his old father hobble in slowly, sighing with impatience as the old man took frequent breaks; on the other side was a pregnant woman, her belly protruding under her hastily-wrapped sari, the *pallu*[7] covering most of her face, two rambunctious children in tow; in another corner was a sickly woman being guided in by a nurse, her face a deathly grey, her eyes holding the truth of her uncertain future.

Hiten watched them all, his mind absorbing the tableau around him yet feeling strangely untouched by it all. He had never invested too much in people, for they had the ability to wound or to leave at will. It was this very detachment that had kept him sane all these years.

"Mr Patel, sir ... what are you doing here?"

Thomas stood in front of him, his brow furrowed with concern.

"Oh, Thomas," Hiten stood up hastily, wincing as his arm twinged at the sudden movement. "I've been trying to get in touch with you. I was worried about Lola."

Thomas took him by the good arm, waving the receptionist's objections away as he walked him towards the Maternity ward. He spoke fast, his words colliding into each other, the 'l's and 'r's even more pronounced, gasping out sentences as though out of breath, his bloodshot eyes and thick stubble revealing the strain of the last few days.

"I did not want to worry you, but Lola had to be induced as they found out she had preeclampsia. The baby was born far too early and she is in an incubator now. We were lucky we got here in time and that there was all the new equipment being installed. Gina is the first baby to be housed in the new preterm baby unit. But she is not good sir. Only 600 gms she weighs Mr Patel. So, so tiny. So many tubes going in and out of her. Poor little thing. Lola cannot bear to see her. She starts crying every time. They are keeping her in because of the C-section. She has not healed fully and we don't know if baby will survive ..."

He came to a sudden stop, his face crumpling.

"The Desai family have been understanding sir, but now they want me to go back to work. How can I? All this ... who will manage ... how to leave ...?"

And then he started to sob, taking large lungfuls of air, as the tears flowed down his cheeks and onto his magnificent moustache, making the hair soggy and causing the handlebar ends to droop.

Taken aback, Hiten patted him on his back ineffectually. He was unused to seeing grown men cry and found this display of emotion upsetting. Then he opened his mouth to offer words of comfort and instead found himself saying, "You go back to work Thomas. I am here. I will take care of Lola and the baby, you don't worry."

Both men were stunned into silence after this, each one wondering how to proceed. Then Thomas took a large white handkerchief out of his trouser pocket and blew his nose loudly and dramatically. Quietly he guided Hiten into the ward, where mothers and babies were housed together.

Lola's bed was in the corner and she seemed to be asleep. It was only as they approached, that Hiten noticed that her eyes were half open.

"Lola, look who is here. Mr Patel! He's come to see us. Look what he brought."

There was a forced jollity to Thomas' voice and Lola turned towards them, listlessly. She tried sitting up, but Hiten indicated she shouldn't. Then he handed her the flowers and said, "Congratulations."

She looked up at him, the tears pooling in her eyes. "Her name is Gina."

"Yes," Hiten nodded and sat on the edge of the bed, tentatively taking her hand in his.

They sat quietly, silence affording them the latitude of private thoughts. Thomas was the first to speak.

"Would you like to see her Mr Patel?"

Hiten looked at him in confusion then realised he was referring to the baby.

"Ahhh, yes, yes of course. Will you come Lola?"

Lola turned her face away. "No," she mumbled, refusing to meet his eyes.

They walked in silence to the preterm baby unit. Baby Gina was indeed tiny, like a miniature doll that could fit into the palm of a grown man's hand. In the incubator, he watched her chest rise and fall, her breathing assisted by a tube inserted into her windpipe, her lungs not yet fully developed.

"How does she feed?" Hiten asked in a hushed whisper, in the largely vacant ward where the lights were kept dim to mimic a mother's womb.

"Right now they are feeding her through the tubes, but they want Lola to express her milk, only she is refusing to do it."

"Why?"

"She feels the baby is going to die."

"What?! Lola is a nurse, she shouldn't be thinking like that! Look at this unit. All this is brand new, the latest technology. This baby has an equal chance of survival here as she would anywhere else."

"I know Mr Patel, but after the trauma of the delivery, the doctors think that Lola has sunk into post natal depression. She is always so tired and sad. After the first few times, she has refused to come and see Gina."

"But she is her mother! She must love her."

"I think she does, but I cannot explain it ... it's like she wants to give herself the pain in advance because if Gina does not survive, it's a pain she will not be able to handle ..."

Just then a nurse came bustling in. She looked at them in annoyance.

"No visitors! Thomas, I told you, don't bring strangers in."

"This is not a stranger, Vanita *ben*[8], he is like a grandfather to Gina."

"Grandfather? I thought Lola was an orphan." She examined him through narrowed eyes.

"Yes, I said *like.* Mr Patel is an old family friend."

"Well, if he is like a grandfather, tell him to get the mother to visit. We want to give baby Gina her mother's milk, there is so much goodness in it that she is missing right now. It will help with her development, her immunity, so many other things."

Thomas looked woebegone. Hiten interjected at this point.

"Tomorrow. I will bring her tomorrow. Will the baby be okay?"

Nurse Vanita shrugged. "It is difficult to say. We are doing our best, but with infants born this early survival rates are not good."

"When I bring Lola here tomorrow, please do not say this. Tell her that Gina is going to live and be a healthy, happy baby."

Hiten surprised himself once again with his assertiveness. He knew that the nurse was only presenting him with the facts, but even as he uttered the words, somewhere within his heart, he knew with an unexpected certainty that they would prove to be true.

It was one thing to say, quite another to do it. His first few days with Lola were unremarkable. His repeated attempts at stilted conversation were futile. Lola refused all offers to walk around the ward, ate little, slept fitfully, and barely responded to the nurses who stopped by. His attempts to take her to Gina were met with blank stares and passive but intractable resistance.

He took to walking down to the preterm baby unit to check in on baby Gina. In time, the nurses started to acknowledge him, some having known him from his previous stay there.

Upon his appearance, they would coo to the baby, "Look, *Dada*[9] is here."

Baby Gina had surprised everyone with her strong will to survive. Day after day she battled infections, weight loss, a compromised immune system, yet emerged fighting. Hiten found himself dreaming about her, this little baby girl grown to a toddler, dressed in a pink frock, squealing with laughter as she exhorted him to push her swing higher, higher ...

Yet, the reality was that she was still combatting all the adversities of having been born far too early, with a mother who refused to acknowledge her existence, let alone give her the sustenance that she so desperately required.

"The baby is doing all she can, but she needs her mother. Lola must hold her, she must have skin-to-skin contact with her. It will help the baby."

Nurse Vanita was only reiterating what Hiten had heard multiple times over. Thomas stood by his side, shaking his head in despair.

"We have tried everything Vanita *ben*. But it's like she has switched off from everyone and everything."

"Then switch her back on! This baby needs her mother."

Then Hiten hit upon an idea. The next day he asked Thomas to bring something over to him. As soon as he was allowed in, he perched himself on a chair by the side of Lola's bed, loosening his sling so that both his hands were level. He took up Lola's knitting needles with the unfinished booties, and attempted to fashion a stitch. He'd often watched his mother knit and figured it couldn't be that difficult. After repeated attempts, and a bit of swearing under his breath, he saw Lola look at him from the corner of his eye.

"What are you doing?" she asked, showing the first stirrings of curiosity.

"Well, I'm trying to finish the booties for Gina. She's going to need them soon, she's getting so big."

He looked up just in time to see a flicker of hope appear in Lola's eyes. She carried on watching his useless attempts without attempting to intervene.

"I thought knitting was easy, my *Baa*[10] and you made it seem so."

"It is easy," she responded softly, "if you know how."

"Then you do it, because I cannot figure this out."

He thrust the knitting needles, the unfinished bootie hanging off it, with the ball of yarn, into her lap. It lay there while she looked down at it, a single tear trickling down her cheek.

"How is she, my Gina? She is getting big, you said."

"Yes, she is. She is a little fighter that one, what a spirit she has. She misses her mother though. You must come and see her."

At this, Lola stiffened and turned her face away once again.

Hiten fell back into his chair, feeling stupid and useless.

THE DOCTOR at the hospital wanted to check how he was healing, so while he sat there being poked and prodded the next day, he asked him.

"What is the cure for post natal depression?"

"You are talking about Lola?"

"Yes. She is refusing to see the baby and everyone has tried convincing her. Thomas thinks she needs to be put on some medication. But I think, if only she holds her baby she will be fine. She will be fine and so will baby Gina."

The doctor looked up from the prescription he was writing, a smile playing about his lips.

"Mr Patel - or should I call you *Dada*? - I think you'll find that Lola and baby Gina have been bonding very well since this morning. Lola has even expressed some milk for the baby. Maybe your knitting idea had something to do with it?"

Hiten could scarcely believe his ears.

"Oh yes, everyone here knows what you have done for the Mathews family. Thomas has been telling everybody that you are a miracle worker. Now, that's all well and good, but you need to keep taking the pain medication and get some rest too. Otherwise, you'll end up as a patient here once again. I mean it. One week at home, no visits to the hospital. Rest!"

Duly dispatched, Hiten was forced to retreat into his solitary existence once again. Yet, his heart felt light with the knowledge that Lola was coming back to normality and that baby Gina would have more than a fighting chance of survival in her mother's loving care.

A week went by and when he heard nothing from the Mathews, his initial euphoria was replaced by despondency. Had he really believed that he'd become an integral part of their lives? Maybe he was better off not interfering, but how could he not? They *felt* like family: Lola like the daughter he'd never had and Gina, the little doll, like a granddaughter that he was desperate to spoil; to shower with affection, sweets and gifts.

He resolved to himself that he would give them time to recover and to heal, to bond as a family, to let baby Gina become healthier. He would reach out again, but perhaps after some time had elapsed, once everything had settled down.

The very moment this was decided, his phone rang.

A frantic Thomas was on the line, his words all a jumble, sounding increasingly desperate.

"What is it Thomas? What are you saying? I don't understand ..."

When the import of the jumbled words finally penetrated, Hiten disconnected, ran up to his room, grabbed the things he needed and called a taxi for the private hospital Thomas had given him the address for.

Twenty minutes later, he wrote out a cheque for 1 lakh rupees as Thomas stood next to him, shaking in terror.

"When did this happen?"

"Two days ago. Everything was going well and then she developed really high fever. The doctors could not diagnose the cause, so they asked me to transfer her here. They said it was sepsis, blood poisoning because of infection in the stitches. She's being given intravenous antibiotics and is on oxygen right now. She barely made it Sir. My Lola barely survived."

"And the baby?"

"Baby is fine, in fact improving steadily. Mr Patel, I cannot thank you enough for everything ... you have done so much for us ... you have been like an angel in disguise ..."

"Shhh, Thomas. It's okay. You need to look after Lola now. She has to get better."

"Sir, I will pay you back. All this money, the hospital bills ... I had nothing except my wedding ring which I pawned, but I promise I will pay you back."

"Please stop Thomas! You focus on Lola. I will go to the Civic hospital and check on the baby, okay?"

Then, almost as an afterthought, he turned around and asked Thomas.

"Is that okay? Can I go and see her in your absence?"

"You are her *Dada,* sir, you need not ask for my permission."

NURSE VANITA LOOKED HARRIED when he saw her. Two more premature babies had been brought in in the last few days and the skeleton staff was barely coping.

"Yes, yes, I heard about Lola. So sad! But she's recovering you say? Yes, that's good. No, put it there, you silly girl!" He jogged alongside her as she shouted instructions to the junior nurses. "How is baby Gina? Well, not so good in the last two days. She was getting better with Lola holding her, but now we have no time to do it ourselves, we are so busy here. She has been quite restless. Where are the charts? I told you yesterday!"

Hiten could barely keep up with her, so frenetic was her pace. Suddenly she stopped short and turned to face him.

"You!" She looked at him appraisingly. "You can hold her. All she needs is human contact for a little while and you could provide it."

"Me?" Hiten's astonishment was rapidly replaced by panic. "No, no. I can't do this. I have no experience with babies. I have never held one in my life."

"So what? There's always a first time. Go wash your hands there. Rupal, get the chair set up, *Dada* is going to hold baby Gina, whether he likes it or not!"

In what seemed like moments, he was in a rocking chair, with a swaddled baby Gina being placed gently on his chest. His heart was knocking so hard in his chest, he feared he'd deafen the baby. With shaky hands he held her against himself as though she were a fragile china doll. To calm himself he started humming an old K.L. Saigal song and found the baby nestling into him. The moment he stopped humming, the baby let out a little wail of protest, so he started up again. With tiny whimpers she settled into him again, eventually falling asleep.

Nervously, he waited for the ordeal to be over. In a few minutes, a nurse relieved him of the tiny bundle, carting her away while he still sat, shell shocked at what had just transpired.

"Well, that was okay, wasn't it? You can come back again tomorrow at the same time." Nurse Vanita would brook no argument and he knew it was futile to even try.

The next day he turned up as ordered, ready and expectant as baby Gina was duly placed on his chest once again. This time, he decided to hum a different song which she listened to placidly enough. His hands didn't shake now, but her tiny, butterfly-like heart-beat still felt like a miracle. This was the same baby who had been unable to breathe or feed without tubes just a few short weeks ago. Now, here she was, laying upon him, listening to his strong heartbeat, her own little heart fluttering as if in response. If this wasn't a miracle, what was?

When Thomas and Lola returned to the hospital a few days later, they could not believe how well their baby Gina was doing.

"All *Dada*'s work!" Nurse Vanita informed them matter-of-factly.

Before Thomas could start with the effusive thanks, Hiten spoke up.

"It is I who should thank you. For so long I lived a selfish and purposeless life devoid of love and meaning. Meeting you has shown me what I was missing. Taking care of baby Gina has been a privilege, one that I hope you will not take away from me."

Lola and Thomas exchanged glances and then Lola came forward shyly.

"We were hoping Sir, if you didn't mind, could we name you as Gina's godfather?"

"Mind? I'd be delighted! A *Dada* and a godfather ... Who would've thought?" Hiten felt like pinching himself, unable to believe his ears.

There were smiles and hugs and tears all around. But Nurse Vanita wasn't done with him yet.

"Oh no, you do not get away so easily! Baby Gina might be ready to be discharged soon, but there are two other babies here who will need daily cuddling."

"Two other babies? What do you mean? What about their mothers?"

"Both the mothers have other children to look after, jobs to return to and mouths to feed. These are not rich people, they are common folk who need to to earn their livelihoods. Much as they want to, they cannot be here 24/7; their circumstances simply do not permit it. But you, Mr Patel, are a retired gentleman, someone with plenty of time on his hands, I imagine. So I am recruiting you as the *Dada* of all the preterm babies here. You will, of course, need some basic training; you will rotate in some of the other departments so you can learn the inner workings of the hospital. Then we will teach you infant CPR and assign you a nurse 'buddy' till you are capable of working independently. There will also be a formal background check done on you. All of this will take a few weeks, but I'm convinced that you'll sail through it quite easily." Nurse Vanita waved her hands as if to show that these were mere formalities, the decision had already been made. "You will be our official 'baby cuddler'. And I have a feeling you will enjoy it far more than you are letting on!"

WHEN HITEN HAD FALLEN and broken his clavicle, he had had no idea it would change his life, so drastically and so much for the better. As Civic Hospital's pioneer baby cuddler, his volunteer hours are now spent cuddling babies who need human contact to mature developmentally. His evenings are spent in the company of his adopted family.

And then there is a little girl called Gina, with her dark curls and her dimpled smile, who crawls up to her *Dada* with an impish smile and bit by bit, holds on to his trouser leg to haul herself up. She sways uncertainly on her feet, only just finding the confidence to stand upright. But when his eyes alight upon her, he remembers the first time that her slight, frail body was placed upon his chest, and he knows, beyond a shadow of a doubt, that she will forever hold his heart in her tiny little fist.

5

THE RETURN

Yamuna stopped attending school at the age of eight. That was all the education she was ever going to get. Because she was a curious little thing, and because she had enjoyed attending the village school and thumbing through the few dog-eared books it housed, she did cry a little. She had liked tracing the large alphabets, trying to make sense of the lines and the squiggles, matching them up with pictures. It seemed to be a doorway into another mysterious, fascinating world.

Then it all ceased because she was also pragmatic, and understood that her place was in the fields with her mother and siblings.

It wasn't until Badri returned from the city that her urge to learn reared its head once more.

HE SWAGGERED INTO THE VILLAGE, all suited up, his thin frame nearly swallowed up in a jacket much too large for him. Hair oiled back slickly, he'd given up wearing *surma*[1] in his eyes, making him look younger than his twenty-two years. The gaggle of children around him grew larger, pulling and tugging at his shiny jacket sleeves. He swatted them off cheerfully. Yamuna stood on the periphery, eyeing him warily.

"*Bhaiyya, bhaiyya*!" Brother, Brother, the children chanted.

"Shoo!" He laughed, "I'll bring out the sweets later."

He caught her eye and beckoned her over.

"Where's Ganga?" He asked, fiddling with his collar and looking embarrassed.

"Sister is in the fields with *Maa*. I only came to fetch their lunch."

"Will you tell her I'm back?"

Yamuna examined him and then stuck her tongue out.

"Tell her yourself!"

His yell was still ringing in her ears as she raced with her little bundle towards the fields.

THE SUN BEAT down a little less fiercely in the afternoon upon the small village of Ramlokpur. It was just another anonymous place within the vast expanse of India. Boasting a population of roughly 1500 inhabitants, its only claim to fame was that once, a holy man with considerable following had passed through. A well had been dug in his honour, and even in the most scorching of summers, the well never failed to provide the village with cool, sweet water. The villagers firmly believed it was his blessings that had ensured the continuous supply, and so erected a temple as well in recognition of him. As no one knew which of the pantheon of Hindu gods he had actually worshipped, they arbitrarily settled upon Shiva, the yogi god. The temple, aside from the Chief's house, was the only solid structure of bricks and mortar. In the mud huts that clustered together like a huddle of old women, lived the rest of the population.

The villagers sat on their haunches, grouped around his solitary chair. Yamuna could tell he was uncomfortable, unaccustomed to being treated this way. She hung back, watching the scene from afar, chewing on the end of her plait.

"So, Badri *bhaiyya*, you make good money in the city?"

"Yes, yes. Very good. The Seth is kind to me. He has even given me a room above his garage to live in."

There was a collective gasp. A room! Their mud huts did not compare.

"I drive his car, fetch his groceries and take his dog for a walk. He trusts me."

"You've done well, Badri!" In strode Kedar, their village chief, a big-bellied, bald-headed man with a booming voice, and clapped his hand on Badri's back, nearly dislodging him from the chair. Someone hurried to bring the *charpoy*[2] over and placed it in the shadiest spot under the *Peepal*[3] tree. "That Master must've taught you well, huh?" he continued.

The villagers mulled this over as they looked between Kedar and Badri. It was no secret that Kedar had loathed the teacher they all fondly referred to as Master*ji*[4]. He had been vehemently opposed to the higher education that Master Raju had tried to impart to the largely illiterate village and Kedar had used every trick in the book to sabotage his attempts - from threats to intimidation to the mysterious fire that engulfed the ramshackle structure they called school.

Yet, a few like Badri had persisted and gone beyond the basic alphabet. And look where it had gotten him!

Unfortunately, Raju had eloped with Kedar's only child Sulekha, and all learning had effectively been replaced by Kedar's incandescent rage.

The timid teacher who had replaced Raju was a lackey, and once again, the villagers learnt no more than signing their names. Once a fortnight, a female teacher came from three villages away to teach the girls the alphabet. It was a requirement by the regional government to appear to be educating the poorest. So, Kedar had pocketed the grant money allotted to the school, and allowed the farce of an education to be carried on in a hastily constructed one-room mud hut that was uninhabitable most of the year.

Now, here sat before him an example of what might have been, if Master Raju had not been sidetracked by love. An upstart who was being elevated and placed on a chair!

Badri knew all too well that his return was not going down pleasantly with the Chief.

He quickly stood up and touched Kedar's feet.

"You are our *Mai-Baap*. Our father, our mother, our protector. How else could I have flourished, if it were not for your blessings?"

Somewhat appeased, Kedar indicated he should sit. Badri wisely chose to squat with the other villagers.

"So, what brings you back after all these years, heh? What has it been - four, five?"

"Four and a half, Sir."

"You're a city lad now. What do you want with us country bumpkins?"

Badri looked down at his feet and mumbled something.

"Speak up!" said Kedar, annoyed.

"I would like to get married."

AND SO IT came to pass. Ganga, the sister that Yamuna had always adored, married her childhood sweetheart Badri. It wasn't without the usual hurdles. Her parents had to provide the dowry, and they had very little to offer Badri. He knew and didn't mind. But Kedar could not allow the opportunity of a wedding pass by without profiting from it. He insisted that Badri be provided a dowry so that the young couple could set up home 'properly', knowing full well that Ganga's parents didn't have two *paise* [5]to rub together. Consequently, they had to take a mortgage outright from Kedar on the last hectare of land they owned. The rest of the land was also already mortgaged to him and this effectively put them in his control forever, just as he'd desired. It was a win-lose situation and all parties got thoroughly drunk in the euphoria of the moment.

"Ey Badri!" Kedar slurred into his ear. "Don't come back, okay? I don't want you giving these villagers any ideas. You got lucky my boy. Not everyone does. Got it?"

For a moment, as Badri looked into Kedar's face, Yamuna saw his mouth pucker, almost as though he was going to spit into it. Then he reassembled his face into its usual subservient set and nodded and smiled.

Yamuna sighed. For once she would have liked to see someone stand up to the Chief, but it was not going to happen. Not in her lifetime.

THEY ALL LAY TOGETHER in a late afternoon siesta after the wedding. Her father snored loudly, and her mother coughed in her sleep. Her two younger brothers slept, curled into each other. She could hear Ganga's breathing deepen as she too slipped into slumber. Yamuna sneaked a peek at her fifteen-year-old sister, still awed that she was now married and someone else's property ostensibly, although Yamuna did not hold much truck with that. Badri was also gazing at his young wife with something akin to pride and wonderment.

"Badri *bhaiyya*[6]," she whispered into the shadowy room.

"Hmmm?"

"Are you still in touch with Master Raju?"

There was a moment's pause, and then Badri answered. "Yes," he said, "Yes - but don't mention it to anyone."

"Where is he? What is he doing? Does he plan to come back?"

"Yamuna, don't be naive. There will be a lynch mob waiting for him if he does. Besides, he is happy. He is teaching in a Government school in the city. He has no plans to return."

"And Sulekha *didi*[7]? How is she? She must miss home. She must miss the Chief."

"I'm not sure Yamuna. I don't interfere in women's business. If she does, that's their problem, not mine."

"Badri *bhaiyya* ... will you never return either?"

He turned and gazed at her a minute before speaking.

"Not for a while, Yamuna. Not while Kedar still holds his grudges."

"Why does he not like you?"

"It's not me he doesn't like. It's what I represent. I represent freedom and opportunity. Something that has been denied to the people of this village."

"Is it because you studied? I want to study. I want to make something of myself!"

"Yamuna, you are a girl. What are you ever going to be? A daughter, a field hand? A wife and a mother? Be content with that."

LONG AFTER THEY had left - her sister and brother-in-law - long after the tears had been shed, the trousseau packed, and the couple despatched by the local bus, Badri's words rang in her ears. A smouldering resentment started up in the pit of her stomach. She did not want to be just a daughter or a wife, just someone's property like her sister had become, in a world where a woman's worth was dictated by her relationship to a man. She wanted more. She wasn't sure *what* that more could be. But she knew that the *how* would only come through education.

Still. There was the dream and then there was reality. Reality was the daily grind of waking up at the crack of dawn, of milking the cows, filling the buckets with water from the well, helping her mother prepare the meagre breakfast for the menfolk, wolfing down whatever remained and then rushing to bathe and change for a day of work in the fields - hours of back-breaking labour followed by more housework before she could fall into a deep, dreamless sleep. Only to wake up and do the same again the following day, and the day after, till eternity seemed to stretch out into one long, hot, dusty, never-ending road.

IT WAS in the month of September that Master Raju returned to the village with his heavily pregnant wife. The Chief's bellow was thunderous enough to frighten the bravest of hearts. At first, everyone thought that Raju would not survive the night. Yet, some of the tears and the pleading of his daughter and wife must have had an effect, for Kedar finally relented enough to house them both.

It was customary for a daughter to return home for the birth of her firstborn child. As Sulekha had been the apple of her father's eye, his rage all but evaporated on seeing her waddle towards him and awkwardly try to touch his feet. Raju was a different story. Cold war ensued between the two men, and some nights Raju would wake up shaking and drenched in sweat, in fear that a pillow was about to descend on his face to snuff his life out.

The baby girl arrived in October, and the celebrations were subdued. *Barfi*[8], a cheaper Indian sweetmeat was distributed in the village, instead of the more expensive and flavoursome *ladoos*[9].

"Had *I* chosen my son-in-law, the baby would have been a boy!" insisted Kedar darkly.

The baby was sickly and Sulekha, never the most robust of girls, found it difficult to nurse or care for her. The rotation of village women who helped soon tired of the scenario and they resumed their own lives and duties. Sulekha sank into a listless apathy. Her mother despaired and begged her husband to hire full-time help.

"Do you have to be so miserly? This is our child, our blood, and she needs help!"

YAMUNA WAS NOT their first choice. She was too young, and despite displaying impressive stamina, she was not the most amenable of creatures. Yet with the Autumn harvest nearly upon them, few families were willing to spare an extra pair of hands. Yamuna's persistence paid off and she was hired for a grand sum of Rupees 350 a month.

"Too much!" Kedar growled but there was little he could do as his wife had trodden upon all his objections.

The bathing and feeding of the child did not seem like work to Yamuna. She was habituated to taking care of her younger siblings.

"You are a natural," Kedar's wife Gulabi remarked as she watched Yamuna oil and massage the baby, who had started to get healthier with each passing day.

"I like babies," said Yamuna, and it was true. But it was only half the truth. She no more saw herself as a field hand than she did as a nanny. Her only agenda had been to get into the household, and somehow, *anyhow,* persuade the Master to resume teaching.

Two months passed by with her barely getting a glimpse of Master Raju. For such a young and dynamic man, he had nearly disappeared inside himself post his return. Fatherhood ill-suited him, and he looked like a lost puppy most times. Sulekha would not hear of returning to the city. So he was caught in a no man's land with nothing to do except retreat into his books, trying at all times to stay out of harm's way.

One late afternoon, however, Yamuna finally managed to corner him.

"Master Raju, you must come and play with the baby. She has started to smile now."

He looked startled. "Has she?"

"Yes, yes. Babies are amazing. Like little sponges. They absorb everything around them. Why, even Sulekha *didi* enjoys her more now!"

"Well ... well ..." He seemed lost for words.

So HE STARTED to sit with his wife and baby more often. Sulekha blossomed once again, and Gulabi, observing the change, would not stop singing Raju's praises to Kedar.

"What a dear little family we have. Look how much he loves her. Would any of *your* prospective matches, those no-good, land-grabbing *zamindars*[10] have taken such good care of our daughter, huh?" Kedar would scowl, look away and then look their way again, secretly touched by the young man's devotion to his wife.

Yamuna smuggled a few of the alphabet books into the house, on the pretext of showing the baby some pictures.

"See how she follows my finger, Master Raju. See? She likes it when I crow like a rooster. Look how she turns to the picture every time?"

She appealed to their pride in their child and saw how quick they were to believe that the baby was no less than a genius. With such subterfuge, she got Raju to start teaching his six-month-old daughter the alphabet. Sulekha would giggle and comb her hair, while Gulabi would snooze on the *charpoy* next to them. Kedar would glower from a distance, reluctant to upset the fragile happiness that had once again crept into the house. Meanwhile, Yamuna would tickle the baby's toes and silently learn as much as she could.

"Sulekha *didi*," one day she mildly inserted herself into a conversation between mother and daughter.

"Yes, Yamuna?"

"Wouldn't it be nice if some of the village children could come to Masterji's lessons? He would feel like he was doing something useful again. And the baby could have some children to play with too?"

BEFORE KEDAR COULD SO MUCH AS RAISE an eyebrow or bellow out a protest, his front yard was converted into a makeshift school with lessons three times a week. Gulabi, his wife, had learned a long time ago that the only way to get around Kedar's temper was to present him with a *fait accompli*. He would then be put in the entirely untenable position of being unable to cut off his nose to spite his face.

Raju's long-suppressed talents were brought to the fore once again. Soon the syllabus included the multiplication tables and a few basic books. History and Science started to get a look in as well. As for Geography, even Kedar would lurk around as Raju expounded on the different continents and the different people that inhabited the world.

"We are only a small dot on this planet. The planet is an even smaller dot in the Solar system ... Imagine how big the Universe is if the size of our village is like that tiny little ant that's crawling up your leg?"

Word spread of Raju's classes, and the villagers started to 'drop by' for a chat with the Chief. Kedar found his house becoming a thoroughfare, and himself becoming some kind of a local hero. Unused to being this popular, he was abashed and alarmed in equal measures.

Things came to a head on the day of the annual village celebrations. Where, in previous times, he would have led the prayers with the local priest and a largely recalcitrant populace mumbling along, this time it was a joyous occasion, with him being *carried* on the shoulders of the villagers to the temple!

"Our village has been blessed by Goddess Laxmi herself!" the village priest exclaimed.

"Saraswati," muttered Yamuna under her breath, for while Goddess Laxmi denoted wealth it was Goddess Saraswati who symbolised learning.

TWENTY YEARS LATER, when a city councillor finally decided to visit the village of Ramlokpur for the waves it had been making in the media, he was astounded to see a flourishing place with three times its population before the education boom. With a 90% literacy rate, the villagers employed the latest agricultural techniques, alongside their own rural experience, and their harvests were rich and plentiful. The young men that left for the cities often returned with funds and acumen, ploughing it back into their own lands, enriching them further. Badri and Ganga were amongst the first to return, happy to shed the frenetic pace of city life and return to a gentler, kinder, more welcoming land than they had grown up in.

Kedar's statue adorned the square. It was freshly garlanded every day and visited once a week by his family. He was widely acknowledged as a pioneer who had recognised the necessity of education amongst the poorest. His granddaughter was a teacher in the local school, which had grown far beyond its humble origins. Master Raju was the much-revered Principal. He remained his unpretentious, good-natured self and still enjoyed teaching the youngest in the school. "Catch them young!" he'd say, and laugh uproariously at his private joke. His own expanding brood had given him life skills that books themselves never could have. He often wondered at the transformation in his fortunes, yet superstitiously, never examined it too closely. All he knew was that his return to the village had been fortuitous beyond his wildest dreams.

The old priest would tell anyone who wished to hear it that it was the holy man's blessings that had transformed the land, returning prosperity and progress to it.

As for Dr Yamuna Jha.

Wife, mother, anonymous patron of Ramlokpur. Stem cell researcher, living and working in the US. Delving into recombinant DNA methodology, finding treatments for hitherto incurable diseases, she was too busy to remember what had rekindled her indefatigable ambition.

Like a comet she blazed on, and in her wake, all else lit up.

6

TOP THAT

"You know you are my best buddies, *na?* Best friends through thick and thin?"

Aman was slurring and swaying as he declared this to the three of us, his hair flopping onto his forehead, his fair skin beaded with sweat. We were drunk too, but not as far gone as him. He was allowed though, his divorce had finally come through and this get-together in Goa had been his idea of a celebration.

The four of us sat outside on his balcony facing the beach. It was early in the evening and the shacks had already started playing a raucous blend of music. All kinds of tourists, Indians and foreigners, milled about on the beach. From shorts-clad foreigners with dread-locks, to sari-clad Indian ladies with anklets on their feet, from rowdy children to placid cows, everyone wandered with impunity on Baga beach. The last-minute plan was met with mostly sold-out hotels, so here we were, in a 'boutique' hotel of sorts, the only place with decent accommodation within spitting distance of a beach.

"Yeah, yeah. Now, come on, sit down or you'll keel over and hit something." Pankaj had always been the responsible one in our group. Responsible for all the mischief, that is. His angelic persona belied an evil-genius mind that had regularly gotten us into hot water at school. Of course, he'd nearly always escaped punishment because no one could ever imagine him doing anything naughty, while the rest of us bore the brunt of his escapades. He sat on the deck chair swirling the whiskey in his glass, glancing up at Aman with a look that was reserved for children who were playing up. Pankaj had thickened in the middle over the years, but his face still had an innocence to it. His wide-spaced eyes and boyish smile made one want to confide in him, and no doubt he was privy to most of our secrets. To his credit, he'd never divulged any.

I guided Aman over to the other chair. "You okay buddy?"

He looked up at me with silent gratitude in his eyes. This was the same boy who had bullied me relentlessly in the first year of secondary school.

"Yeah, bro, I'm good."

The truth was that he wasn't good. Gita had been his college sweetheart and none of us, least of all him, could have anticipated the two of them breaking up. He was dishevelled, distraught and prone to bouts of weeping. We'd been listening to his saga for the last twenty-four hours and our patience was starting to wear thin.

Mahesh sat on the fourth deck chair, cracking his knuckles, observing the sun on the horizon. He was the quietest of us all, the most studious too. The one who'd moved to the US and made his millions. Yet, there was a silent unhappiness to him, as though he'd tasted the life he'd been yearning for and found it unpalatable. We'd thought he wouldn't come, but here he was, over ten thousand miles away from his home, present in body, but so very absent in mind. His hair had thinned in the last few years and his chocolate-brown complexion had taken on a greyish hue. He looked haunted and tired. He'd been quiet most of the time, allowing Aman to ramble without censure. I wondered what was bothering him so.

And then there was me. The unlikeliest member of this foursome. While Aman had always been the good-looking sporty one, Mahesh the academic and Pankaj the charming but naughty one, I was a little bit of everything and a whole lot of nothing. Unremarkable-looking, not particularly bright or athletic, I had always been a shy introvert.

Why after a long first year of picking on me and bullying me to the nth degree, they had suddenly decided to absorb me into their group, I never figured out. But I was very glad for this friendship. It had tided me over so much. They were the brothers I'd never had - crazy, wilful, needy sometimes, remote at others, but always there. Ready to have my back as I was theirs.

I looked over to the pile of discarded beer bottles in the corner. We had been drinking steadily for the last eight hours. Last night's hangovers hadn't even had the time to hit, before Aman had handed us a bottle each at breakfast. My stomach was rumbling now, ready for food as lunch time had come and gone with none of us noticing.

"You know the worst of it?" Aman carried on, as though we'd been following his train of thought, "She said I'd stopped her from finding herself! Finding herself? What does that even mean? And why couldn't she find herself in the marriage? Why go back to slogging over books, ignoring her husband and children; to prove what?"

"Maybe you should have let her complete her Masters degree before getting married." Mahesh said this softly, almost apologetically.

"Why? She's never needed to work a day in her life! What good would that degree have done her? We have enough money for generations to come."

This was true. Aman had been born with a silver spoon in his mouth. His family owned a textiles business that had grown with every generation. Aman had never needed to worry about work, he'd always known there would be a job waiting for him at the end of his education.

"Speaking of work," Pankaj looked over to Mahesh. "How's it going Stateside, with the economic downturn and all?"

"Yeah, it's not really affected our sector much. People will always need medicines, won't they?"

"Hmmm, so they will. Big Pharma will continue to thrive. How's Malathi's father now?"

"He was given six months and he's managed a year. He's sick of the chemo though and wants to stop and just ride it out. The family is trying to persuade him not to. But I kinda agree. Where's the quality of life in all of this, man?"

The talk was turning dolorous and it wasn't helping Aman's mood in the slightest.

"Hey!" I said, "fancy playing that old game?"

"Which one?" Aman frowned at me.

"You know ... the most embarrassing moments of our life ... that shit!"

"Oh yeah!" Mahesh seemed to perk up at the memory. It was a game he'd invented when we were in our last year of school to relieve us of the tedium of studying for our exams. It had been such a success and constant source of laughter, that it had become something of a ritual between us. Every few years when we managed a meet-up, we'd play the game, each time with hilarious results.

"Great idea, bro!" Pankaj looked at me approvingly.

"What's the theme of the day then?"

"Work!" Aman chimed in. "Our most embarrassing moments at work."

"Not fair, Aman. What embarrassing thing could have possibly happened to you? It's your own damn company!" Pankaj was laughing as he said this, but there was an edge to his voice, one I'd never heard before. Was something going on with him too?

"Hang on! It's not *my* company, it's the family's, and why, do you think I haven't messed up in my time? In fact ..." A dreamy look came over his face and for a minute or two he seemed to disappear into himself.

"Helloooo ... Earth to Aman, where are you?" I poked him in the ribs good-naturedly.

He looked at me and grinned, his eyes still slightly glazed.

"Do you remember Miss D'Souza?"

"Your dad's hot secretary, the one with the magnificent bosom?"

"Yes ... that one. This story is about her."

He sat back in his chair, feet on the table in front of him, his arms crossed behind his head, elbows sticking out. Aman was still a handsome man, even with his slight paunch and receding hairline, but as a young boy, he had been irresistible.

"She joined the office when I was around thirteen years old and only just starting to notice girls. She was pretty well-endowed, you remember right? And she always wore those tight tops that stretched over her chest."

All of us nodded, our minds travelling back to our teens and our first crushes.

"Well, I think she knew the effect she had on the men around her and I think she quite enjoyed it too. The problem was that she was actually a really good secretary, extremely efficient and besides, her English was fluent, which was handy when dealing with foreign clients. So, much as mummy and the *chachis*[1] wanted her fired, *dadaji*[2], daddy and the *chachas*[3] wouldn't hear of it."

He took another swig out of his bottle.

"From a very early age, I used to go to the office every Friday after school, remember? It was an informal way of learning the business, something my father and his father had also done. But after D'Souza had joined, I would mostly go to stare at her and her cleavage. She took it in her stride, I guess she was used to it."

"Now, bear in mind that all of this happened before Gita entered the picture, okay?"

"Okay, okay, whatever you say. Just keep going." Pankaj was lounging back in his chair, his knee shaking of its own volition.

"Over the next few years I managed to convince myself that she had fallen in love with me. She always gave me a chocolate bar, or bestowed me with a special smile, and you know how, as boys, we'd read meaning into the most insignificant of gestures. Well, at nearly sixteen I decided that she was the woman I was going to marry."

"What?! How old was she anyway?" Mahesh guffawed aloud.

"Nearly thirty, I'd imagine. Anyhow, that Friday I decided that I was going to propose to her. But for a proposal, you need a ring. Since I had no access to mummy's jewellery which she kept safely stowed in her locker, I decided to raid *dadaji's* room."

It was my turn to be shocked. "Your grandad! What on earth were you thinking? Did he possess diamond rings?"

"The point, bro, is that I wasn't thinking. I just wanted a ring and my grandad had one of those big, ugly, calculator rings with the different stones that some *jyotishi* [4]had told him would bring him luck. But he'd leave it lying around, often forgetting to wear it. So I thought it would be perfect for the job."

"I hid it all day in my school bag, and after playing a particularly rough game of football, all sweaty and dirty, I rocked up at my dad's office."

"D'Souza was there, looking as cool as a cucumber in some green top and skirt she was wearing. She looked up at me and smiled, then pulled out a Cadbury's bar from her desk drawer. I stood there shaking like a leaf, not knowing how to go about proposing in front of the forty other people who sat in that large room."

Mahesh leaned forward. "Well? What did you do?"

"I asked her to come over to the water cooler. She looked quite perplexed, but thought that maybe I wasn't feeling well, so she followed me there."

Aman looked at the beach, a rueful smile on his face, reliving the scene in his mind.

"The water cooler was situated in a long, narrow corridor that ran parallel to the main office, but at the end of the corridor was *dadaji*'s office, which he rarely occupied. By this time, most of the business was being run by my dad and the *chachas* anyway. So, I got down on my knees near the water cooler and held out the ring, stammering out an absurdly passionate proposal to her. She just looked flabbergasted. So, to reiterate my ardour, I pulled her down and tried kissing her. Just then, guess whose door I see opening at the other end?"

"No way!"

"Way, bro, way! *Dadaji* caught me red-handed trying to stick my tongue down the office secretary's mouth, who was at the very least, a decade older than me. The fact that I had pinched his ugly, calculator ring was just the icing on the cake!"

He shook his head again.

"It didn't end well. I was thrashed to within an inch of my life and banned from coming to the office for the next few months, till poor Miss D'Souza left of her own free will. It was not a happy time in my life, I can tell you that now, even though back then I was too embarrassed to ..."

As we fell about laughing, he simply grinned at us and said, "Top that."

❧

THE CHALLENGE HAD ALWAYS BEEN to tell a tale that was wilder, more embarrassing and cringe-worthy than the one before. It was my turn.

"I had only just graduated from University with a Political Science degree when I got hired by the charitable arm of The Ignatius Foundation."

Mahesh nodded because he remembered dropping me off at the interview on his motorbike.

"My job, amongst other things, was to take the visitors we had from abroad to all our far-flung projects around the country, in the hope that we could impress them enough to eke some foreign funding out of them."

"I'd been working there about eight months when Mr Nigel Williams arrived from London. His company had sent him on some sort of fact-finding mission to ascertain whether we were worth the investment or not."

"I really couldn't have had an easier gig. I mean, this guy was a total Indophile. He loved everything about India: the food, the culture, the colours, everything. I think he would have happily signed off any amount to us, but his bosses wanted to see proof of our projects in black and white, so it became my job to show him around."

"The project I picked was a village on the outskirts of Punjab. We had given the village *panchayat*[5] some funds to improve upon the irrigation system for their farming, and I wanted Mr Williams to see how well the village had been doing ever since. A local family had agreed to host us for the day, and so we set out from Chandigarh where we'd stayed overnight, not by taxi or car, oh no, but by a local bus. Mr Williams wanted to experience India firsthand, the way an ordinary person would."

"Are you mad? A *gora*[6] on a local bus, with all the pushing and shoving and hanging off the roof! What did he make of it?" Aman asked.

"Well, actually, the people were really nice to him. We Indians still have a bit of a colonial hangover, so they couldn't have been sweeter or more accommodating. He wasn't pushed or shoved, they parted like the Red Sea for Moses, offering us a seat, but pressing close to us. And they stared ... a lot. But that didn't bother him. We chatted away quite happily on our four-hour journey there."

Pankaj poured himself another whiskey. "Then what happened?"

"Not much really. Everything was going well. Mr Williams was impressed with the irrigation system we'd helped set up, he loved the welcome he'd received from the villagers and then it was time for lunch."

"Oh no, I think I know what's coming ..." Mahesh shook his head sorrowfully.

"Nah, it's not what you're thinking!" I countered. "You'd think it would be him, but it was actually me. You guys know that I've always had a sensitive stomach and I react badly to lactose. Well, guess what we had for lunch that day?"

"What?"

"*Makki ki roti aur sarson ka saag*[7]. With lots and lots of *ghee*[8]."

"Oh man!"

"How could I refuse? Here was this foreigner, lapping it all up, asking for seconds. How could I be fussy?"

"Don't tell me your stomach fell out?" Aman asked.

"Wait for it ..."

Now I had everyone's attention as they leaned forward, urging me to carry on.

"We were taken on a tour of the village after lunch, shown the local school which really was one small room with coir mats and an ancient blackboard, but the villagers were really proud of it, and I could see that their enthusiasm was infecting Mr Williams. I knew then that I had it in the bag."

"Then my stomach started rumbling. I asked where the toilet was, fully expecting to be pointed towards the fields. But, oh no! They had just had a brand new Indian style toilet installed in the village and couldn't wait to show it off to us."

"The whole lot of us trooped towards the toilet, which was a *pukka*[9] structure made with bricks. There was a partially ajar door leading into the room, and a small washbasin on the outside, which already had a rusty water stain on it. We all peered inside the room and the stench! The stench was so bad it made me gag. But that wasn't the worst of it."

"Why? Was it really dirty?"

"The entire toilet looked like it had been made with black tiles."

"Black tiles? Who uses black tiles?"

"They weren't tiles, they were flies! Every conceivable surface was covered in flies and they were moving. The whole room seemed to be humming and swaying, while also stinking! I saw Mr Williams take a step back, he was so shocked. I felt my own butt cheeks clench so hard that my urge entirely disappeared."

"Yuck! And the villagers?"

"Well, those poor folk didn't know there was anything wrong. They had a new toilet, but didn't know that it had to be cleaned regularly to keep it hygienic."

"As we walked back, Mr Williams was quiet and contemplative. Then he started talking about maybe investing in another project, one that would educate villages such as these about sanitation and hygiene. Shell-shocked, I kept agreeing with everything he had to say."

"So, now you were getting funding for two projects. How is that embarrassing?" Pankaj scoffed.

Mahesh gave him a look. "Let him finish."

"I'm not done yet. We took our leave from the village, and despite the disgusting toilet, we couldn't help but be impressed by how kindly we had been treated by everyone. Once on the bus, I started to relax, and boom, my stomach started its *tandav*[10] again!"

"Couldn't you have stopped off somewhere and gone to a proper toilet?"

"Where? We were in the back of beyond! So, I just got more fidgety and tried to keep myself distracted by really focussing on Mr Wiliams' stories. He was talking about all the projects his company had funded, the far-flung places he'd visited and the extraordinary capacity for generosity that the humblest of people possessed."

"Under normal circumstances, I would have truly enjoyed a conversation like that. But, my mind kept circling back to my stomach, and the effort was just getting too much! Beads of sweat broke out on my forehead and I started praying that I'd last the journey, but it was not to be ..."

"What do you mean? Did you ...?"

"Yeah man, I shat my pants."

"What?!"

"I thought it was only a tiny fart and I let it out, but the worst happened. I shat my pants. Then I sat there like that for three hours, pretending nothing had happened. Mr Williams sat next to me, stony-faced, not saying a word. People on the bus couldn't work out where the smell was coming from and kept trying to inch away from us, thinking it was the *gora* who stank to high heaven. It was the most torturous and mortifying journey of my life."

"Did you get the funding?"

"Oh, he was as good as his word. He sent us the funding for both projects, but he also sent me a pack of Marks & Spencer underwear in the office post. People were mystified by the contents of the packet, but I nearly died of shame!"

Everyone's mouths had fallen open and I picked up my beer bottle and took a swig out of it, watching the sun set in all its multi-hued glory.

Then I said, "Okay, go ahead and top that."

"I'M HUNGRY," Pankaj declared, looking into his empty whiskey glass.

"How dude? That story was gross! How can you be hungry after that?"

Pankaj shrugged and my stomach rumbled in response.

"Let's order some room service guys!"

"How about some *saag* with *ghee*?" Aman looked at me and laughed.

I picked up the cushion on my chair and threw it at him, missing him by a whisker. Mahesh was already calling and ordering on our behalf. He'd always stepped up when the rest of us behaved like juveniles.

"What did you order?" Pankaj looked at him inquiringly.

"When in Goa, eat Goan! I've asked for some prawn balchao, vindaloo and cafreal, with a side order of rice. It'll be about forty minutes. Time enough to tell my story. Another round of beer?"

"Hang on! I've got some peanuts somewhere!" Aman staggered into the room, returning with two packets of roasted peanuts. We settled down once again, passing the packets between us, munching noisily, wondering how Mahesh could possibly top my tale.

"I had been working at my firm in the US for over two years at this point, and although I had many acquaintances, there was nobody that I would have really called a friend. I was that typical lonely nerdy Indian guy who was good with numbers, but socially awkward to the point of being completely isolated."

"My clothes didn't help either. I wore the same greys and browns that I had always worn in India. There was nothing fashionable or even remotely modern about my clothing. I dressed like my grandfather and didn't see anything wrong in it. Clothes and shoes had always been utilitarian to me, I only came to understand their significance and their impact much later in life."

I studied Mahesh, with his designer specs and his Abercrombie & Fitch T-shirt, and for the first time marvelled at just how subtly he had altered himself over the years. He looked and smelled expensive, as though he'd stepped out of some high-end designer catalogue.

"Anyway, at this time, there was a big hubbub at work. One of our Directors was planning to visit and everyone had gone into overdrive in an effort to impress him. He was quite an old fashioned man of Austrian descent, and a real stickler for smart appearance and top-notch performance. Everyone was a little terrified of him. As I was still a very junior member of the team, I was given sundry tasks to perform, because there was no way that I was going to come into contact with a bigwig like that."

"You should have seen the place, man! Everything was sparkling clean, everyone was suited and booted, all the relaxed dress codes thrown out of the window. Even I was told to put on a suit and tie for the day."

"The only suit I possessed was the one that my grandfather had given me before I left India. It was a brown checked number from the 70's and the sleeves on the jacket were much too short on me. The trousers were also a bit tight, but I figured that from a distance it would look fine. So on the day, I think it might have been a Tuesday, I turned up at work, looking like some throwback from a 70's movie, all wide collars and bell-bottomed trousers, with an orange shirt thrown in for good measure."

Mahesh shook his head as though still embarrassed by his sartorial choices all those years ago.

"The looks I got! But people were polite and didn't say much, although I think there were quite a few sniggers that I was blissfully unaware were directed towards me."

I passed the peanuts packet over to Mahesh and he took a handful, chewing thoughtfully, chasing it up with another sip from his beer bottle before he continued.

"The Director was being given a tour of the offices, and at one point he walked through ours too. I thought he was quite handsome, in an ageing Marlon Brando kind of way. I could see why people were so petrified around him, even the normally laidback Americans; he just had this no-nonsense aura about him. Not one to suffer fools gladly, I thought to myself, and then promptly forgot all about him after he'd passed me by."

He paused for a moment, as though reflecting back on his younger self.

"It was late afternoon, and by this time the suit felt really itchy, so I took off the jacket, left it on the back of my chair and made my way to the toilet."

"Oh no! Not another toilet story ... you guys are determined to put me off my food!" Aman made a face at Mahesh.

"Shut up Aman! Just listen," growled Pankaj.

"I just needed to pee buddy, not do a number two like our friend here." Mahesh grinned.

"Anyway, I went into the employee toilet that was rarely frequented because of its location. I'd often go there to get away from people, and most of the time, I'd have it all to myself. Not on this occasion though. Somebody was already in one of the cubicles, having an almighty dump from the sounds emanating from there. Man, the sound effects were something else! I unzipped my fly and stood at the urinal, letting the past two hours of coffee and water gush out of me, when the door to the cubicle opened and out walked Mr Director. I'm not sure what thought crossed his mind, but both of us just stood there, staring at each other open-mouthed in the mirrored wall. Then he turned slightly pink, nodded at me and went to wash his hands at the basin."

"Sounds to me like this was more embarrassing for him, than for you," noted Pankaj drily.

"Hang on, I'm not done. I was so nervous and taken aback to be in the same room as the man that I finished peeing hurriedly and yanked the zip up in a panic. That's when it happened."

"What happened?" My curiosity got the better of me and I leaned so far forward that I fell off the chair in my inebriated state.

"Careful buddy!" Mahesh helped me back on, while the others threw peanuts at my head.

"I got my dick caught in the zip!"

"Ouch!!" Aman winced in sympathy while the rest of us stared at Mahesh in horror. There is truly no worse fate than harm coming to our privates. Every man knows and understands the pain and humiliation that accompanies any such horrific happening.

"I must have screamed so loud that Mr Director spun towards me, startled out of his skin. Then he saw what had happened and came over. The next few minutes were the most mortifying of my life, but at the time all I could think of was the pain, and how to extract my foreskin out of the unforgiving metal teeth of the killer zipper. To his credit, he tried his best. He pulled gently, I screamed in agony. Then I tried pulling, while he tried breaking the zip, but nothing seemed to work. Somewhere in my mind was also the thought that the top boss had his hands on my penis!"

Pankaj had already started to laugh while Aman and I were squirming in sympathy.

"What did you do then? Did you manage to extricate yourself?" I whispered, my voice still strangulated from the image Mahesh had conjured.

"Nope! After a futile ten minutes of trying, Mr Director got me to put on his roomy jacket, to cover the source of my agony and embarrassment and called 911. He also insisted on accompanying me to the hospital. Never a more painful or ignominious journey have I ever had in my entire life. But Mr Director showed an entirely new side to himself by being the calmest, most reassuring person I could've asked for in such a crisis. Several of the office people had volunteered to go instead of him, but not once did he leave my side."

Mahesh looked out at the ocean, pausing for a beat.

"Once in the ER, I was dealt with swiftly, by a young Indian doctor who poured mineral oil over the site, left it to soak for a while, and then gently removed me from my zipper. Needless to say, I was bandaged and given sedatives to help recover from the trauma. I didn't go in to work for an entire week after that, too mortified to face people, wondering what sorts of jokes were making the rounds. But Mr Director had obviously had a word, because once I did go back, no one ever referred to Zipper-gate in front of me, although I heard much later that it was quite a popular topic amongst my colleagues."

"Phew! That's quite a tale." Aman was nodding in sympathy.

"Hey!" Pankaj said suddenly, "was that where you met Malathi? That young Indian doctor? You'd always said you met in a hospital, but never how."

"Haha ... Bingo buddy! That's where I did meet her and am I lucky, she still consented to go out with me after that." Mahesh smiled at him. "Okay I'm done, time for you to top that!"

THE FOOD ARRIVED JUST THEN, and the room service boy wheeled in the trolley to the sound of our excited cheering. We tipped him handsomely and sent him on his way before attacking the food with combined ferocity. It had been a good twelve hours since our last meal, and the first morsel of the delicious Goan food tasted like manna from the heavens.

The beach shacks had amped up the music, and rock numbers were now competing with popular Hindi songs. But nobody seemed to mind. From our vantage point on the balcony, we watched the beach front get even busier as night drew near.

"We really should check out the beach, guys! Can't believe we've been holed up in the hotel for over a day without stepping out." My remark was met with nods and grunts, the rest of them too focussed on the food to think of anything else.

Aman licked the curry off his fingers then turned towards Pankaj and said, "You know I'd happily lend you the money. Why are you going to a bank?"

Both Mahesh and I were nonplussed. This was the first we'd heard of Pankaj needing anything, he'd always been so self-sufficient.

Pankaj shrugged and looked at us. "Sorry guys, I just asked Aman to be a guarantor and all he wants to do is lecture me."

"What do you need the money for?"

"To buy the house off my brother. Papa left it jointly to us in the will, hoping we could carry on living under the same roof, but Pritam's wife ..." He shrugged again, not saying any more, but we all understood.

Joint families were the utopian ideal the previous generations had striven for, and to some extent, even managed to implement. But in our day and age, with everyone craving independence and privacy, it was a failing concept, creating unnecessary strife and rifts within families. Clearly Pankaj was the latest casualty.

"Is Pritam being difficult?" Mahesh probed cautiously.

"No, not difficult, just realistic. For him to afford a place in South Delhi, he has to get a good price for his half of our property. Of course, we could both sell it and buy our separate places, but I can't bear to part with the house I grew up in. Too many memories."

"Don't get attached to bricks and mortar, man. It's just not worth it. The memories will go with you wherever you go." Mahesh said. "But if that's what you want to do, I'd be happy to loan you the money too."

"Me too," I mouthed quietly, although I was probably the least comfortable financially, but if one didn't step up at a time like this, what good was a friendship of thirty years?

"Thanks guys!" Pankaj sounded choked up, although we couldn't make out his expression in the dark, the room light being behind him. "But I'd rather not mix friendship and finances. It always ends badly."

Now I understood why there was a strange kind of tension about him. I would be having a word with him later, he always listened to me.

"Do you want to hear my story or not?" He asked gruffly.

"Wait, wait! I've got something else in my bag for afters." Aman got up to go inside again.

"No drugs dude! I'm too old for that crap." Mahesh looked at him.

"Drugs? Who wants bloody drugs when you've got this!"

Aman came out brandishing a small tin box which he opened to reveal four beautifully wrapped *paans*[11].

I grabbed mine, greedily biting into it, immediately being transported back to school days and orange mouths; the sweetness of the *gulkand*[12] with the sharpness of the *choona*[13] and the crunch of the *supari*[14].

"Is your local *paanwala*[15] still alive?" I mumbled with a full mouth, trying to swallow the juices that had collected on my tongue.

"No, his nephew took over after he died, but his *paans* are just as good, you should see the queues that line the block at night."

"Mmmm." Mahesh was mollified, chewing on his *paan*, looking at Pankaj to begin his story.

"So, back when I was still a trainee hotelier studying Hotel Management, we had to spend a certain amount of time in each department, learning the ropes as it were. My favourite was Food and Beverage. I got to eat all the delicious *khaana*[16] the chefs prepared, right at the source!"

I could well believe that, for Pankaj had always been a foodie and his tall, rangy frame had become meatier over the years owing to this.

"My least favourite was Housekeeping, where the Head Housekeeper would follow me around to make sure I completed cleaning a room in the allocated forty-five minutes, with the corners of the sheets folded just so."

"You had to clean rooms? You never told us this!" Aman looked at Pankaj open-mouthed.

"Nothing wrong with cleaning rooms, you *ameer baap ka ameer beta*[17]. We do all our cleaning and cooking ourselves in the US. You're just spoilt with all the household help you have here." Mahesh pronounced this calmly, looking at Aman who grinned back, refusing to be provoked.

I didn't say anything because I had no idea how to cook or clean either with Medha, my wife, handling that side of things. That's how I'd been brought up, but I knew things were changing as the newer generation of Indian women wanted men who were more handy around the house.

"Can I continue?" Pankaj asked.

"Yeah, go on bro."

"This incident actually occurred when I was assisting at the Front Office. That's where the Reception, Concierge and Guest Relations are located."

"Isn't that also where the prettiest girls worked?" Mahesh looked at Pankaj, smiling in a knowing way.

"Yep! That's where I got my heart broken the first time around."

"What was her name? Didn't she leave to fly for Cathay?"

"Her name was Sonam and she joined Emirates dude. But that's not the point of this story."

"Was she there when the 'incident' happened?"

"Yes, she was. Okay, maybe there was an element of trying to impress her as well, but really man, you've got to let me carry on ..."

We nodded in unison, each of us relaxing back into our seats, legs stretched out, appetites satiated, feeling the warm glow of satisfaction that comes from the assurance of being amongst people who know you and love you, despite your flaws or your circumstances.

"At the front desk, we'd often have people drop off packages for guests who were expected to arrive within the next week or so. We'd check the guest's reservation and then make an entry into the log book. When the guest checked in, we'd inform him or her of the package, hand it over and cross it off in the book. Easy peasy."

His knee jiggled again, a nervous tic that he must have acquired recently.

"Except that sometimes, the guests would be no-shows, as in, they just wouldn't turn up. In those instances, we'd wait for a while in case they made another reservation, and if that didn't happen, we'd try and contact the person who'd left the package in the first place in order to return it. If, for whatever reason, we couldn't, we'd hand it over to the manager who would deal with it appropriately."

"What does that mean?"

"Well, a lot of times, it would just get thrown away, especially if it was edible stuff sitting around for that long. If it was more valuable, I think the managers would make a decision on what to do with it. Most times though, it was pretty ordinary stuff like letters or invitations or boxes of *mithai.*[18]"

He leaned back in his chair again, running his fingers through his hair, a rueful look crossing his face.

"This one time, a package had been sitting around for quite a while. It was addressed to an American guest by the name of Mr Wesson, who did not arrive as per his original booking. The package was held onto for another few weeks, when Mr Ganesh, the Front Officer Manager decided that we needed to clear out the store room and get rid of all the unnecessary rubbish cluttering up the area. I was given the task, along with another employee by the name of Vivek. It was boring work, checking outstanding packages against the log book entries and against any future reservations, then opening and discarding or setting aside the packages. We were about halfway through when we came across this package. It had been left by some German dude by the name of Mr Schindler."

"How do you remember the names so clearly?" I asked.

"Only because I was reading a thriller at the time in which the hero used his Smith & Wesson revolver a great deal, so the name just stuck in my head. Also, we'd just had Schindler elevators installed in the new wing of the hotel which was still under construction and again, that name just stuck as well. With what followed, the names were branded into my brain forever. "

I nodded in understanding, indicating that he should continue. Word association has always helped me remember names as well.

"Anyway, this package had been sitting with us for over a month. So I took the executive decision of opening it. What I found inside was so underwhelming that for a minute or two, both Vivek and I were completely dumbfounded."

"What was in it?"

"A whole lot of rubble of what seemed like rocks or bricks."

"Huh??"

"Exactly! Then, after coming up with various ideas, we surmised that it must be an April Fool's joke. We were already in the month of May, and Mr Wesson had been booked in for April. Vivek asked me whether there was any point in tracking down Mr Schindler to return the package to him. But I decided no. Who would want their joke returned to them unpackaged? So, in all my wisdom, I decided to chuck the package and consider it a job done."

He looked around, grinning at the confusion on our faces.

"About two months later, Mr Wesson arrived and asked for his package. At this point I was already working in a different department, but I was summoned to face Mr Ganesh. Luckily for me, Vivek was off sick and couldn't squeal on me. Mr Ganesh was furious because the package could not be found, but in our haste and haphazard handling of the log book, we hadn't crossed off the entry either. So, everyone had been searching high and low for this damned package."

"What the heck was in it?"

"Hang on! Let me tell you what happened next ..."

Now we were intrigued and hanging on to every word, just the effect Pankaj was going for.

"When Mr Ganesh told me what was in the package, my head spun! I knew I'd have to do something if I wanted to save my skin and my job. So, I gave him some crazy excuse, saying I'd go find the package, that it must still be in the store room, just hidden in plain sight and all that. Then I raced off, my mind formulating and discarding various plans, till a wild idea presented itself to me."

He chuckled at the memory.

"I grabbed a large airmail envelope, roughly the same size and dimension as what I remembered, scurried across to where the new wing was being built, picked up bits of bricks and rubble, shoving them into the envelope, ignoring the curious looks the labourers were giving me. Then I raced back to the store room, found a quiet corner and wrote out the names in as illegible a handwriting as I could manage with my left hand. Twenty minutes later, I presented the package to Mr Ganesh, sweating bullets, but pretending that it was all a big misunderstanding."

"Did you get away with it?"

"What did Mr Wesson say?"

"What was in the original package?"

We bombarded him with questions and he held up his hands, as if to ward us off.

"Okay, okay! One at a time. Firstly, yes, I did get away with it. I never heard what Mr Wesson said, but he must have been satisfied with the contents of the package. I held on to my job and my skin, and as you can see, I'm very capably managing a hotel as a General Manager today."

We nodded in unison, still waiting to hear about the package.

"Finally, what was in the package? Only the contents of the most important historical event of the year before, if not the entire decade: the rubble from the Berlin Wall! Which I threw away unwittingly, and substituted with the rubble from our hotel."

He watched our mouths fall open, then leaned back and grinned at us knowingly.

"Now, top that."

We sat in silence, digesting the fact that some poor American dude had been palmed off the contents of an Indian construction site as rubble from the Berlin Wall! We were struck by a sudden stone-cold soberness at the thought of this great con being perpetrated by one of our own, wondering how the heck he'd gotten away with it. But then again this was Pankaj we were talking about. Pankaj, the evil genius. We sat there knowing beyond a shadow of a doubt that he had most definitely won this round.

He winked and splayed his hands innocently as though absolving himself of all crimes and misdemeanours. Mahesh guffawed suddenly, "You crazy dude! You're lucky no one ever found out or your ass would've been grass."

Aman just kept looking at him wonderingly. "How? Just ... how?"

I chuckled, looking around myself. Whatever our worries, our burdens or heartaches were, this bonding was integral to each one of us. This game, this silly confessional game had a strange cathartic quality to it. Who knew who would top it the next time around - but this one had definitely gone to Pankaj.

And since none of us could really surpass that tale, we took ourselves off to the beach for a dunk in the sea and revelries that would last for a while yet.

7

FUNK

2006

"NONE of your Indian Princess act here, my girl. This is a toilet brush. Learn to use it!"

It had been two days since I'd arrived in London, and clearly, Mrs Jhunjhunwala, or Auntie JJ as I addressed her, wasn't impressed with the skid marks I'd left in the bog. She handed me the toilet brush and bustled out, every fibre of her being conveying irritation. Slowly, I inserted the brush in the pot and swirled the bleach she'd poured in. The smell made me gag, and a little tear made its way down my cheek. Where was Ratna *bai*[1] when you needed her?

"Really Gul, it will be a wonderful experience. You'll become more independent. Learn to navigate a foreign city on your own. Think of all the fun you'll have!"

Mummy had certainly sold it to me. What she'd omitted was that I'd be stuck in a tiny flat with an eccentric Parsi woman and a flatulent poodle. Said eccentric was taking off for France on her annual girls' (girls my foot! They were all over seventy!) meet, and I was to be caretaker of flat and poodle for (gasp) an entire two weeks! Before she left though, Auntie JJ was putting me through my paces. From making sure I dusted everyday (where was the dust?), took Chi-chi (flatulent poodle) for his daily walk, to going grocery shopping to the local Sainsbury's, and of course, keeping the bog clean and smelling of (yuck) lavender.

Really, Auntie JJ wasn't an ogre. She was just particular. And peculiar.

Of course I knew why Mummy was eager to send me 4000 miles away. It was because of Farhan. She'd hoped distance would kill the budding romance between us. What she didn't know was that the romance had blossomed and withered already. I wasn't going to tell her either. Pride and sadistic pleasure lay somewhere behind my hazy strategy.

So, although I hadn't exactly jumped at the prospect of living in London for a bit, I hadn't dismissed the notion out of hand either. Distance would be a good thing. I could lick my wounds, or maybe find someone else to temporarily lick them for me.

There were still two days to go for Auntie JJ's departure though, and I hoped I wouldn't suffocate to death by then.

Aside from the bric-a-brac that overpopulated her tiny flat, Auntie JJ insisted on keeping the heating on full blast, and the windows shut at all times. Admittedly it was December, and the air was colder than a witch's tit, but I could've done with breathing and being able to smell something other than lavender, body odour or dog fart. Every evening, after our dinner of roasted cod, mashed potatoes and mushy peas, Auntie JJ invited me to imbibe a little sherry with her. Every evening I refused politely. I would then sneak into the bathroom, crack open the window, breathe in some London fumes, and exhale the smoke from my sneaky cigarette.

I was bored senseless, and since Auntie JJ hadn't dipped her toe into 21st century things like mobile phones and wifi, I was at a complete loose end too. I could choose to watch vile daytime television with her, listen to her snort over the Daily Mail everyday, or read the horrendous Regency romances her place was littered with. I chose none of the above, choosing instead to sulk in my room, planning all the naughty escapades I'd get up to while the cat was away.

Chi-chi, the old dog, seemed to sense my restlessness. He took to following me around the cramped flat with an expression that amounted to, "I know what's on your mind, and I don't like it." He'd whine and scratch at my bedroom door if I had it shut, then promptly deliver a silent, deadly fart as a present as soon as I opened it. I hated that dog. I think the feeling might have been mutual.

On the eve of her departure, Auntie JJ solemnly handed me the keys to the flat, and a list as long as my forearm.

"This is the first time I have allowed anyone to stay here since Persis, my niece, died," she sniffled a bit. "I hope you won't let me down, my child. Your mother said you are a very responsible girl."

A pang of guilt at the unholy thoughts I'd been having made me lean forward and embrace her. "You have nothing to worry about Auntie JJ. I'll take care of everything."

Later, I aired all my clothes for fear that I'd end up smelling as fusty as her.

THE THING about Farhan was that he was just so damn handsome. All chiselled face and grey eyes and musculature to rival a race horse. Religion didn't come into it. Not for me anyway. I just wanted to get laid and he was the best candidate for it. Mummy would've been horrified if she heard me speak this way. I was the '*good girl*', with the '*bright future*'. I had no business entertaining such thoughts. Except that my raging libido thought otherwise.

At twenty-one, most of my girlfriends had lost their virginity yonks ago. So, why was I still unpackaged?

We'd nearly made it. Ayesha, my sweet, understanding, soul-sister of a friend, had made herself scarce, lending us her bedroom when her parents were at work, for us to indulge in our usual heavy petting session. His hand had crawled under my top and I'd arched my back towards him, hoping he'd take it further this time. He'd groaned as I touched him. "Let's do it Farhan!" I'd whispered, slyly unzipping him.

"What? No. NO! Stop it Gul!! What's wrong with you?"

"What's wrong with *me*? What the hell is wrong with you?"

He'd leapt off the bed. "I'm saving myself for marriage. You know I'm engaged to my cousin Anjum. You've always known."

"Bloody hell, Farhan! I'm not asking for your hand in marriage. I'm just asking for a fuck!"

He'd looked shocked and backed away. "I can't do that ... my religion won't permit me to sleep with another woman ..."

I'd laughed then. "So, have we been knitting beanies and discussing politics all these weeks? Grow up, Farhan!"

He'd walked out at that point. Sanctimonious, hypocritical jerk!

THE BLOODY DOG had to sniff every nook and cranny. It took him twenty minutes to decide where to wee and another ten on where to poo. I tugged at his lead, and he just gave me a baleful look.

It wasn't like I didn't try to make it up with Farhan. I thought it was a lovers' spat. He thought worse. Much worse. When the sniggers on campus became obvious, I'd asked Ayesha for an explanation. She wouldn't meet my eye. After much hemming and hawing she finally explained, "They think you're a nymphomaniac."

I nearly spat my coffee out at that!

Nymphomaniac? Chance would be a fine thing!

I tugged at Chi-chi's lead again. He came along this time.

"Hey, you! Oii ... lady!"

I turned around to gaze at a strapping six-foot-two ebony god who looked distinctly unhappy.

"Yes?" I tentatively enquired.

"You gotta pick up the dog's poo, yeah?"

My gaze followed his to the deposit on the pavement. Chi-chi had done his mistress proud, and produced the loosest, smelliest, ugliest poo of all time. I shot the dog a filthy glance, and reached for the bag inside my pocket. What a disgusting practice this was. Couldn't I just leave it there to organically decompose, like people did in India?

"You must pick up after Chi-chi, Gul. You will be fined if you don't. It's not just etiquette, it's the law." Auntie JJ had drummed this repeatedly into my head.

Yuck, yuck, ghastly.

"You not from around here, I can tell. Where you from?" he drawled at me.

"Mumbai." I mumbled, desperate to get away, and get rid of the hot mess in my pocket.

"India? Haha. Chicken Tikka Masala!"

Very funny, I thought, doing a mental eye roll. I started to walk away, but he fell in step with me. He probed, I dodged. Talking to strangers had never been my forte. Besides, my head was still full of Farhan and all the unspeakable things I wanted to do to him, post rumour-mongering.

"I'm David. What's your name?"

Fed up, I looked him right in the eye and said, "Gul Batliwala. Nice to meet you David. Goodbye."

HE WAS WAITING for me the next day and the next and the day after that too.

Soon, we established our own little routine. He'd wait for me at the street corner. I'd pretend not to see him. He'd saunter up to me, with his big toothy smile and loose limbs. I'd studiously ignore him the first five minutes and reluctantly hand out tidbits of information the other twenty five. I actually started to enjoy our brief encounters, as they were possibly the only highlight of my otherwise tedious days.

Christmas shoppers were out in full force. Carols were blaring everywhere. London was grey, sullen, festive and expectant, all at the same time. Old memories of being here with Mummy and Daddy as a child crowded in from time to time. Happier days, more innocent days. Days before Daddy's affair with his secretary had come to light.

"Gool, why you so gloomy all the time?"

Gloomy? Me? I plastered a fake smile on, and looked at him. "It's called Parsi melancholia."

That stumped him.

"Come out for a drink tonight? Just you and me? I'll cheer you up."

I looked at him assessingly. I had to admit he had grown on me. He was handsome, charming and loquacious. Not the brightest button or the sharpest tool, but hey, who needed IQ in bed?

I OPENED ALL the windows of the flat. Lit multiple candles and fragrances sticks. Dusted everything within an inch of its life. Threatened Chi-chi with decapitation if he so much as pointed his rear in my direction.

David was coming over this evening. This could be the bravest or the most foolhardy move of my life. What did I know of the guy anyway? He could be a rapist or a serial killer.

Well, at least I wouldn't die a virgin!

SADE WAS on repeat on the CD player. The wine was chilling. The crudités were on display, and I had my sexiest underwear on under a Christmas jumper on which Rudolph's nose lit up every five seconds. I applied a little lip gloss, and gave myself a once over. Not bad. Not bad at all. I wasn't vain, but knew that I had inherited my father's coltish legs, and my mother's sensuous lips. Shame that Farhan had no use for either.

Christmas was two days away and four houses across the street, someone had gone to town with the decorations. All manner of illuminated fauna dotted the front lawn. Father Christmas hung precariously off the chimney, whilst his sled blinded anyone foolish enough to look at it directly. It was all in such poor taste that I didn't know whether to shudder or applaud.

When the doorbell rang, I felt a shiver go through me. This was it. This could be the night.

David stood at the door in a black jumper and black jeans, carrying an enormous bunch of flowers in his hands. His teeth were in such stark contrast to the rest of him, that a giggle nearly escaped me.

"I got the dog some treats."

Ahh, that was sweet. Chi-chi obligingly walked up, sniffed him, wagged his tail desultorily and walked away.

"Dog got the melancho thing too?"

Huh.

I poured him some wine, arranged the flowers in a vase, and then positioned myself close enough to smell his aftershave.

"You're a real pretty girl but you don't say much."

"Not much to say," I reparteed, giving him my sexiest glance.

It didn't take him long to slide over and slide his tongue into me. This guy could kiss and how. From gentle nibbles to doing it *a la francaise*, he ran the entire gamut. I slipped my hands under his jumper to feel the hard muscle of his torso. He returned the favour. We groped each other till exasperated, I took off my jumper and threw it aside. He grinned at the sight of my red bra. Nope, no virginal misgivings for this one.

Things were getting hot and heavy when I first heard the sound of someone choking. I sat up abruptly, pushing David off me.

"What was that?"

"What?" he mumbled, trying to push me back down.

"Listen!" I commanded.

We both listened. There it was again. A strangled choking sound. Chi-chi!

The dog was choking on one of the treats that David had kindly scattered on the floor for him. Panicked, I ran over to Chi-chi and started hitting him on the back. Chi-chi carried on choking. Could one perform the Heimlich manoeuvre on a dog? I was certainly going to try! I picked Chi-chi up and tried knocking the breath out of him by squeezing his stomach hard.

"Hey Gool! You're going to kill the dog ..." David looked horrified at the sight of me in my undies, stomach thrusting a choking poodle.

"Help, you useless man!"

"How?"

"Dunno! Call 999 or something!"

"They don't come out for dogs."

The argument was moot anyway. Chi-chi had only just gone limp in my arms. The dog was dead.

"Gool, I think the dog's dead."

No shit, Sherlock.

NOTHING like a dead dog for buzzkill. To give the devil his due, David did make some half-hearted attempts at foreplay. But Chi-chi's body, covered with a sheet in the corner, finally got to him.

"Gool ... I, ah, got to go now. I'll see you around, yeah?"

I nodded dispiritedly.

Shutting the door behind him, I pondered my predicament. What does one do with a dog's body at 11 pm?

I got very little sleep that night. First I disposed of the evidence i.e. the treats that had killed poor Chi-chi. Then I looked for the list of instructions and numbers that Auntie JJ had left me. Finally, I ruminated on the possibility that I was jinxed as a person and as a woman. I mean, which flippin' God had I pissed off?

"UNHELPFUL COW," I muttered as I slammed the phone down.

The 23rd of December is not the day to ring a vet's and ask for help. The receptionist clearly had her mind on the impending festivities rather than on providing any useful information to a distraught dog killer.

She'd listened in silence as I'd explained the situation.

"Well, you could bury him in your garden."

"I don't have a garden, I'm in a flat. Listen, could you please send someone out to collect the body. If you could house Chi-chi till his owner gets back, I'd be most grateful."

"Sorry, we don't have enough staff for that. You could bring the dog to us. We're not too far."

"Yes, but I don't drive and I don't have a car here. Please, is there any way?"

"You could take the tube."

At this point I'd hung up.

Tears of frustration sprung up in my eyes. Poor old flatulent Chi-chi, lying in the corner, stiffening up with rigor mortis, sent my guilt into overdrive. I started to bawl my eyes out.

After fifteen minutes of self-pity, I calmed myself and went looking for a carrier to put Chi-chi in.

DEAD DOGS ARE DEAD WEIGHT, I soon found out, as I lugged the travel holdall to the tube station. Every ten paces, I had to take a break and switch hands. Of course Auntie JJ had taken the good case with wheels on her holiday. I'd found this old holdall filled with photo albums at the back of her wardrobe. I'd left the albums lying on her bed, taken all the mothballs out, and placed them like a charm around them.

Then I had spent a good hour trying to cram Chi-chi into it.

Hauling him towards the station, I wondered how I would explain this fiasco to Auntie JJ. She'd adored the dog and I'd killed him. Well, not killed him with my own bare hands, but certainly with my negligence. Some dog sitter/ houseguest I'd turned out to be!

Having purchased my ticket, I made my way to the right platform. A dozen stairs confronted me. I took a deep breath, and started my journey down. I'd made five stairs when the burning in my arm made me stop and take a breath. Two young lads passed me by. They looked at me, said something to each other, then turned around to come back.

"Need help with that, sweetheart?"

I nodded gratefully. "Yes please. If you could just take it to the bottom of the stairs, I'll take it from there."

They grasped a handle each and started to carry it down. See, Farhan? Chivalry isn't dead. I followed them down slowly. The only trouble was, they didn't actually deposit the holdall at the bottom of the stairs. Instead they carried on at a good clip.

"Hey! Hey!!!" I shouted, but they just jumped into the train as it pulled away.

I stood dumbfounded.

I guess I'd just been robbed. Of a dead dog.

Who could I report this to? What could I say? I sat on the steps, laughing and crying at my predicament. It could only happen to me! At that moment I vowed to give up on my futile endeavour of ridding myself of my hymen and instead become a nun, renouncing all worldly temptations! Maybe then I would receive forgiveness for poor Chi-chi and my appallingly self-absorbed behaviour.

2017

Parsi melancholia is easily overcome by Punjabi *joie de vivre* and three children. Needless to say, I didn't stay a virgin forever nor did I become a nun. When Sanjay barrelled into my life, with his loud personality, his never-say-die attitude and his big Punjabi *luddies*[2], I barely had time to catch my breath, before being hooked, booked and cooked by this gorgeous *Punju* hunk. Even Mummy couldn't find fault with him and despite wanting a Parsi boy for me, overcame all her misgivings to bless our union. However, Auntie JJ never forgave me for the death and abduction of her dear Ch-chi and to her I was *persona non grata* for the rest of her life. Can't say I blamed her.

Twinges of regret still catch me unawares, particularly when I get a whiff of something funky and fetid. Poor Chi-chi! What an ignominious exit he had from the world! What must the thieves have thought upon uncovering their loot?

Now, when my kids beg me to get them a dog, I remember the Chi-chi saga, and demur. “I don't have a good history with dogs,” I say cryptically. Only Sanjay knows the whole story and he catches my eye and guffaws each time. I guess I’ll never live that one down.

Maybe ... we'll just get a cat.

8

LOST AND FOUND

Maybe if Dr Seth had not strayed from his routine, none of what followed would have happened.

He'd returned later than usual that night and not found a parking spot close to the house. The locality was jam-packed with cars of all sizes. These days, almost every household had two to three vehicles, and since there were no designated parking spots, people just grabbed the nearest one, parking haphazardly without any consideration for another motorist or resident. But that's the way things were in recent times. People were getting more selfish and more insular. The price of progress.

Dr Deepak Seth was a child of the '50s, a post-independence era that had been filled with optimism, self-belief and values that Mahatma Gandhi had preached: tolerance, non-violence, integrity. Sadly, 70 years later, those values were being steadily eroded in a land that had grown increasingly intolerant and violent, with a moral compass that swung erratically from day to day towards materialism and selfishness. It was a world he no longer recognised, for the most part.

So he'd parked the car far from the house, setting a mental reminder to move it closer later, when all the shoppers and visitors to the surrounding eateries had left. He had an early morning visit the next day to a patient who lived in Dwarka. An old patient who'd been loyal to him for over twenty years, and now, as he lay on his deathbed, Deepak felt it was the least he could do to go see him, even though medicine would do him no good now.

"*Dua karo, dawa nahin,*" he'd advised the family members gently the last time. What he'd meant was that prayers would ease his suffering far more than medicines would, at this late stage. They'd accepted his advice but insisted he still visit, as he was far more than just a family doctor to them. He was a friend, a counsellor; in fact, he was a part of the family.

None of this seemed odd to Deepak. Even in a fast-paced, rapidly changing environment, some things stayed the same - the warm congeniality of the people, for one. The fact that he was a doctor was secondary to being human, to being a person who was so much more than just a title ... He liked it that way. He liked the fact that there was still warmth and hospitality; a free flow of emotion, a blurring of lines, an ability to empathise, to give and receive help graciously. It was this that kept him hopeful. While the daily news would have him believe that the world had gone mad - and indeed he saw it too, in the many infinitesimally small things he was surrounded by to the many larger things he encountered daily - there was still something good that lingered in the land. Like a perfume worn by a beautiful woman who'd only just left the room. There was hope and promise in it.

It was past midnight when he remembered he had to move the car. There had been a spate of robberies lately, and since one of the car's doors didn't lock, he was worried somebody would break into it, parked as it was in a remote, badly-lit part of the locality. There was nothing of value in the car, but the potential damage an unsatisfied robber could do, was enough to make Deepak get out of bed hurriedly, dropping his medical journal to one side.

"Where are you going?" Deepti asked him. She was watching another Shahrukh Khan movie late into the night.

"I have to move the car."

"Leave it. It's so late now, why are you bothering?"

He ignored her question, putting his jacket on and unlocking the main door. Sometimes he wondered if his sister had any idea of what went on outside the house. Ever since her foot had been amputated, she never ventured out. Her entire world consisted of the maid who came to clean and cook daily, the *sabziwala*[1], who was kind enough to bring the vegetables to their door every day, and the neighbours who dropped in for *chai*[2] and *gupshup*[3]. It was a sad existence to be handicapped in this way, but she'd never controlled her diabetes as he'd repeatedly warned her to, and here she was.

It was dark and quiet as he hurried towards the car. The streets were deserted, except for the few stray dogs that wandered about as if it were their own fiefdom. The street lights cast a bright glow around them, leaving pockets of darkness in between. The air had a definite chill to it, as autumnal days were sliding into winter.

He'd just celebrated his birthday mid-October. Seventy-three. He couldn't believe he was this old. His body was still lean and nimble, his mind still sharp. The only indicators of his age were his grey hair and the pouches under his eyes, a legacy of years of insomnia and studying thick medical journals. People commented on how young he looked, like a man in his fifties. That appealed to his vanity. Nidhi had always ribbed him about how vain he was. Like a peacock, she'd said, watching him strut in front of her full-length mirror.

A dull ache returned unbidden. How had he managed to live twenty years without her? He could still hear her voice, remember the touch of her hand, feel her presence amongst the saris that lay unworn in the wardrobe, recall her laugh from the P.G. Wodehouse books scattered around the house. Yet, she wasn't there, not really. She was long gone to a place he hoped he'd join her in someday. He knew she was waiting for him.

So many thoughts crowded his head as he walked in the dark. That's probably why he didn't see them. They were practically upon him when he first registered them - three men with their faces covered.They'd tied scarves over their mouths and noses so that no one could identify them.

"Hey, *buddhé*[4]!" The first one knocked into him, while the other two blocked his way. He knew immediately that this was bad news.

"*Paise nikaal*[5]." The first one, presumably the gang leader, commanded him to hand over his wallet.

Deepak felt his knees buckling under him. The other two grabbed him, leading him to a bench. As they sat him down, he quickly slipped his car keys under his thigh. Mentally he cursed himself for not having listened to Deepti. He rooted around in his jacket pocket retrieving his wallet.

The first one grabbed it out of his hands, rifling through the contents quickly. The other two grabbed his cellphone and then made him hand his watch over to them. Even in the lamplight it was hard to make out any of their features, but he spotted a long snake tattoo on the forearm of the leader. From their voices, they didn't seem to be older than their late teens.

"*Beta*[6], I'm a semi-retired doctor. I don't have a lot of money. You are welcome to whatever is in the wallet."

One of the boys slapped him around the head.

"You think we're asking for permission?"

"Stop it!" The leader said quietly, taking out the wad of notes. "He's just an old man, there is no need to hit him."

Deepak slumped back into the bench, hoping against hope they wouldn't spot the keys.

"What else do you have on you uncle? Any gold chain?"

Deepak shook his head. He had never owned a gold chain. Whatever gold he'd ever bought had been for Nidhi, and after her, it had passed on to her daughter, Nikita, who lived in Hong Kong. What would an old man like him do with gold anyway?

"He's wearing a ring." The third member of the gang had just spotted his wedding ring.

Oh no, not that! Deepak's heart sank as he realised they expected him to turn his ring over to them. He took a deep breath and addressed them.

"*Bete*[7], you look like good boys from good homes. Why are you doing this? You have taken the money, no? This is the only thing I have of my dead wife. Please don't take this from me."

The third member laughed - a short, sharp laugh. "What, do you think we are - a charity? '*Please don't take this from me*'. Shut up and hand it over!"

"Wait, wait ... here, here's my car keys. Take my car. It's parked down there. Please, just leave me my ring."

They took the keys, one of them despatched to check the veracity of his claims, while the other two stood guard over him. He returned shortly, jogging back.

"It's an old Maruti junk heap, not worth the trouble."

"Well, uncle," the leader spoke again, his voice a quiet rasp, "thanks for the offer, but I think we'll take the ring instead."

He threw the keys back at him and held out his hand, palm facing upwards. Deepak hesitated, then saw the glint of a knife in the second member's hand. Slowly he struggled to take the ring off his finger, begging Nidhi's forgiveness internally. He placed the ring in the upturned palm, a deep sadness overwhelming him. For thirty years that ring had been a part of him, a reminder of a brief but happy marriage, and now that had been taken from him too.

"Okay, let's go."

"What about him?"

"Leave him. He's not going to do anything."

"No calling the police, okay? Or we'll find you and kill you."

He shook his head sadly. He'd never intended to call the police anyway.

They melted away just as suddenly as they had appeared. He stayed seated on the bench, feeling the quiet night pressing down upon him. He felt lost suddenly, and old, so old. It was like losing Nidhi all over again.

They'd all said it wouldn't last. She was older than him, a divorcee with a teenage daughter. But the moment she'd walked into his clinic, his heart had done a somersault. At thirty, he'd been half-willing to settle down into an arranged marriage, but all that had flown out of the window the moment he'd set eyes on the statuesque beauty who'd been referred to him by a former patient. They were doctor and patient, to begin with, then friends, then lovers and after many, many years of opposition, objections, dismay, denial and recalcitrance, finally husband and wife. How much time had been wasted in persuading others that love did not recognise age, culture, background or any of the petty differences that separated people! How much of that time could have been better spent loving one another? Especially, knowing in hindsight, how limited that time really was. Still, he was glad he'd had her, for however long he did.

Now, the one symbol of her that he'd carried on him at all times had been wrenched off him too. He didn't blame the boys, he didn't blame fate or life, but he did blame himself. He had wanted to secure a car that was worthless, and in turn, lost the last valuable thing he'd had left.

He didn't know how long he sat on that bench, maybe he even dozed off for a bit. Then, the slightest breeze ruffled his hair from the back and he felt as though someone had lightly planted a kiss on his head. Startled, he jumped up from the bench, turning around just as quickly, only to stare into inky nothingness.

At home, Deepti had fallen asleep on the sofa, the remote still in her hand, no doubt worrying about his whereabouts. Shahrukh Khan was singing on screen, his arms stretched wide, a song pregnant with the meaning of life. Deepak paused for a minute to listen to the lyrics: "*Life changes every second, from joy to sorrow, from sunshine to shadow; Live every moment to the fullest, enjoy the day for what it brings, for you never know whether there will be a tomorrow.*"

Then he switched off the television, brought a blanket out and tucked it in around Deepti, letting her sleep where she was and quietly went to bed himself.

DIWALI WAS APPROACHING AND SUDDENLY, the entire neighbourhood was in the grip of a festive fever. People were getting their houses repainted, new clothes were being purchased, the *halwais* [8]were busy making sweetmeats and the naughty locality kids had already started letting off *patakas*[9] despite the nationwide ban on them. The air had a smoky, hazy quality to it and Deepak finally felt ready to put the entire episode behind him.

He had not intended to tell Deepti, but the first thing she'd noticed was the absence of his wedding ring, and the entire tale had come spilling out of him. Before long, everyone around them had heard of the 'bandits' who had looted poor Dr Seth. People had come over for endless cups of *chai*: to sympathise, to caution, to extrapolate.

"What a cruel world we live in, where even an old man like you is not spared!" This from Mrs Vaidya who was only two years younger. He'd bristled visibly and left the room to visit the toilet, not to return till she'd left.

"I've been hearing that no one is safe on the streets! We'd better start locking our doors during the day as well. Who knows how bold and brazen these men can be? They may break-in in broad daylight too!" Mr Bannerjee's words of warning fell on deaf ears. People were so accustomed to wandering in and out of each other's houses in the day, it seemed ridiculous to curtail their activities because of a few random thefts.

"I've been hearing different things," Shyama the maid squatted next to Deepti as she whispered this. "Some say they are a gang of Bihari servants, but others say that they are boys from well-to-do families, robbing people because they want the drugs." Deepti leaned in, fascinated. "What else do they say?"

Deepak was not interested. As far as he was concerned, the boys/young men/Bihari goons had at least spared him his life and limbs. He had no fear of dying, but worried about Deepti. How would she manage without him around?

His morning clinic had been slow lately. Not many people seemed to be falling sick, or maybe they were just postponing their doctor's visit till after the festival. His usual good advice about eating healthy, exercising and getting enough sleep was at odds with what most people were doing at this time of the year. They'd be overindulging in sweets, getting very little exercise and subsisting on a few hours' sleep every night after their *taash* [10]parties. He sighed to himself. It was the same every year. After Diwali, there would be an influx of patients queuing up to see him.

As he sat in his little clinic, which wasn't too far from home, he pondered over how long he would carry on. Deepti had been urging him to retire ever since he'd turned seventy. Retirement was such an alien concept to him. You retired from work. Medicine - the treatment and healing of people, had never seemed like work to him. It was, and had always been a vocation. How could he stop doing something as natural to him as breathing?

There was a knock on the door. Shruti, his secretary, came in.

"There's a new patient to see you today Dr Seth."

"Oh, what's the problem?"

"Actually, it's a father and son. Apparently, the son's had a sore throat he can't get rid of. Father, by the name of ..." she consulted her notes, "Mr Sudhir Naik has brought the son, Suhel, with him."

"Okay, send them in."

This was probably a case of laryngitis. But he would need to check the boy properly before he diagnosed him.

The father and son walked in a few minutes later. He was surprised to see that the boy was not as young as he was expecting him to be. This was almost a young man, with slight stubble and a shy, diffident manner about him.

"Dr Seth, I have been trying to get him to come to you for over a week now, but he keeps refusing. He's practically lost his voice and we've tried everything from saltwater gargles to *Disprin.* There is no fever, but college work has been hard and he's been working so many nights at his friends', studying all night long, it's taken a toll on his health."

"Right," Deepak nodded, looking at Suhel who kept his head bowed, too shy to even meet his eyes. Probably one of those boys who was overpowered by his father's personality.

"Take off your sweater, young man, let me check your chest."

He took his stethoscope from behind him. Suhel shrugged off his sweater reluctantly, and Deepak spotted it straight away. The snake tattoo was unmistakable, regardless of all the other clues he had missed.

He kept his face deadpan as he checked his chest and back.

"No congestion as such, so I think this is just a bad case of laryngitis. His voice needs a rest, as does he. This all-night studying is not really helping him at all."

Deepak returned to his seat.

"So, Mr Naik, have you lived in the area long?"

"No, we just moved here three months ago. We were in Pune before this. My job is a transferable one."

"I see. Where are you from, originally?"

"Nashik, but we haven't lived there in a long time, although that's where our ancestral home is."

Deepak was used to engaging his patients in conversation. He firmly believed that treatment wasn't just about physical symptoms, but also about psychological and emotional ones. Oftentimes, people would reveal a lot during a casual conversation, which helped him plot a course of medication that was suitable to their particular ailment. He never just treated the one thing, he treated the entire person, tailoring the medication, adjusting the dosage, customising it to the individual and not the condition.

"How many other members in your family?"

"Just one younger daughter who is fourteen, and my elderly mother. My wife died last year."

Deepak noticed Suhel wince as his father said these words.

"I'm sorry to hear that, particularly when you have teenage children who still need their mother. Was she very ill?"

"Ill? Oh no. My wife committed suicide. She had been suffering from depression for many years." Sudhir Naik looked numb as he said this, as if he still hadn't processed the fact of her death. As if vocalising it so cavalierly would show that he was dealing with it even though, deep down, he really wasn't.

Suhel got up suddenly.

"Can we go now Pa?" His voice was just a hoarse whisper, but Deepak recognised the quiet menace in it. Only now, he sensed the quiet desperation too.

"Yes, yes. Thank you for your time, Dr Seth. I'll pay outside."

"No, please don't bother, it wasn't any trouble at all. Besides, I didn't prescribe any medication to you. You're on the right track when it comes to treatment. Rest is the best remedy. And if you need to talk, I'm here. Don't ever hesitate."

Then he looked Suhel in the eye and said, "No late nights for you, young man. Sometimes, the only way to heal is to let time take its course."

He didn't expect to see or hear from the Naiks ever again, so was surprised to see Suhel loitering near his clinic a week later.

"Hello, young man! How are you? Feeling any better?"

Suhel nodded then followed him inside. Shruti still hadn't arrived and Deepak felt a moment of disquiet. What if he was knifed here? Would anyone know who had done it, or why? Then a sudden sense of calm descended on him. If this was how he was meant to go, then so be it. At the other end, Nidhi would be waiting and he was ready. Deepti would never have to worry about money, he'd left her enough. Nikita had promised to organise everything for him as per his wishes. So this was as good a time as any.

He turned to face Suhel, ready for whatever fate had in store for him. Instead, he found him on his knees, sobbing quietly.

"My dear boy, whatever is the matter?"

He kneeled down next to him, awkwardly putting his arms around the frail body that shuddered as he cried. They stayed like that for what seemed like hours but was probably only minutes. Then he sat back and let the boy collect himself, handing him a handkerchief to wipe his face.

After a while, Suhel looked up at him and said, "Thank you."

"For what?"

"For not telling my father. I know that you know, but you didn't tell him."

Deepak stood up.

"I have no idea what you're talking about Suhel. But I'm glad you're feeling better. Have you been gargling with saltwater?"

He turned his back to the boy, busying himself with the papers on the cabinet behind his desk.

"Dr Seth ..."

"Hmmm?"

"I have something I need to return to you."

He turned slowly, cautiously, wary of letting hope blossom in his heart.

The same upturned palm held his wedding ring out to him. Before reaching for it, he studied Suhel's face. Then he put his hand over it and asked, "Are you sure you don't need this more than I do?"

Suhel shook his head, his body slumped in defeat.

Deepak took the ring from his hand and replaced it upon his finger. The deep indentation had been a daily reminder of the ring's absence. Now it settled back into the groove, as though happy to be back home.

"Can I ask you something *beta*?"

Suhel looked at him blankly, waiting for him to continue.

"Are you angry with her?"

"Who?" It was a whisper, a tentative stalling.

"Your mother. Are you angry at what she did, leaving you the way she did?"

Suhel looked down at his hands, not answering, but his wiry frame had started to shake again.

"Sometimes," Deepak carried on as if not noticing, "I get angry with Nidhi too. That's my wife who died twenty-odd years ago. I get angry because I think she betrayed me by leaving me early, by falling sick and not recovering. But when I think about it, what could anyone have done, beyond a point? Death comes to all of us, sooner or later."

He helped Suhel up from the floor, guiding him to the chair. Then he poured him a glass of water.

"Your mother's illness was one of the mind, not visible like a physical ailment would be, but equally corrosive and debilitating. Perhaps she saw death as an escape from her pain, not as a betrayal of you, just as a way out?"

Suhel looked up at him, his expression unfathomable. Then he spoke slowly, as if unused to the thoughts he was vocalising.

"I wanted to study medicine too, to become a doctor like you. Then, after she went, I stopped studying. I dropped out of medical college and joined a vocational one. That's where I met ..." His voice trailed off, as though realising he'd said too much.

"Your 'friends'? The same ones you've been on a robbing spree with? Has it brought you any peace, any happiness?"

Suhel swallowed, looking shamefaced. He looked away, then looked back at him.

"I saw you that night, long after we'd robbed you. I saw you sitting there on that bench, looking so spent and alone. I felt bad, really, really bad." He looked down at his hands again. "Dr Seth, I don't know what to do ... I feel so lost ..."

"My dear boy, nothing is lost. You are still very young, there is still time to make amends and to change direction, if you so choose. But first, you have to allow yourself to grieve. You have been stuck in a cycle of anger for way too long, you have forgotten that the only way to heal is through acceptance of your loss." He paused, a sudden image of Nidhi laughing revisiting him. "Remember, those that we love are never truly lost to us. They exist in some form, somewhere, maybe in another realm, waiting to see us when we're ready to leave. But while we are still here, we have to make the most of our lives, our precious lives. By running amok, by your destructive behaviour, you are doing nothing but wasting all your potential."

Deepak leaned forward on his desk, looking at Suhel intently.

"Go back to medicine. I think you'll find that in helping others you will help yourself the most."

❧

Dr Seth was eighty-five when he finally retired. He'd outlived his sister, he'd outlived the pesky Mrs Vaidya too. He didn't really feel his age right until he turned eighty-four. Then the arthritis kicked in and going up and down the stairs became increasingly difficult for him. Nikita had tried to relocate him to Hong Kong, but he was happiest in India, in familiar environs, rapidly changing but still holding steadfast to the culture and heritage that defined her.

When he died at the ripe old age of eighty-six, just a few short months after he'd retired, his young partner, a certain Dr Suhel Naik, performed all the last rites, just as a son would. As he had predicted, it was in medicine, and in being of service, that Suhel had finally laid his demons to rest and found the one true thing that he would love his entire life.

Dr Seth had always reiterated that while mankind can be stupid and selfish, cruel and callous, we also have an immense capacity to be kind, generous, altruistic, forgiving, empathetic and loving. Happiness, true happiness, lies in following an unselfish path - in giving rather than receiving, in returning to life much more than life has handed to us. It was a philosophy he had followed in his own life, a philosophy he'd handed down to Suhel, and one that Suhel tapped into daily.

He even refused to remove Dr Seth's name off the board that hung outside the clinic they'd shared for the last six years. To this day, each time he looks at that board, he sends up a silent thank you to his mentor and friend, the man who saved him from himself.

THE END

❧

Sign up today to hear of Poornima's new releases and promotions!

AFTERWORD

Word-of-mouth is crucial for any author to succeed and if you found this book interesting *please* do leave a review on Amazon and Goodreads. Even if it's just a star rating or a sentence or two, it would make all the difference and would be very much appreciated!!

If you enjoyed this book, you can sign up to hear more about my new releases and any special offers!

Do visit www.poornimamanco.com to keep abreast of all my news.

ALSO BY POORNIMA MANCO

Parvathy's Well & other stories

Damage & other stories

The Intimacy of Loss

Twelve - stories from around the world

Parvathy's Well & Other Stories: The India Collection

A Quiet Dissonance

ACKNOWLEDGMENTS

This book would not have been possible without the tremendous amount of feedback that I received from my readers. Having tired of my sad and gloomy tales that examined the underbelly of life, they urged me to write something funny, heartwarming and uplifting. This took me out of my comfort zone in so many ways, challenging me to put a positive spin on stories that I may otherwise have written as quite dark or depressing. In the process, I found that yes, life is full of laughter, hope and joy, if we seek it out proactively!

A shout out to my amazing Advance Reader Team (ART), who sifted through my manuscript and found errors that had slipped through the earlier edits. Their response to my stories was a great gauge telling me that I was moving in the right direction with this book. If you'd like to be a part of my ART, drop me a line at poornima@poornimamanco.com.

Another big thank you goes out to my wonderful editor, Charulatha Dasappa. She makes me re-examine my ideas continuously; polishing and refining the thoughts till there is a laser-sharp clarity in my mind about what I am presenting to my readers.

Team Miblart has once again brought a wonderful cover to life. The saffron and turmeric colours are meant to represent India in her most beauteous and festive mood. And of course, the book begins and ends with two of India's most famous and celebrated festivals: Holi and Diwali.

This book is also a tribute to my birthplace. Whereas in the former two books, the predecessors to this one, I highlighted the many inequities, injustices and fault lines that India contains, in this one, I attempt to showcase the beauty, the culture, the spirituality and the heritage that defines her as well. A sum of many parts, India constantly defies description. She can only be felt deep within one's soul, her touch feather-light, her voice a soft whisper, containing the wisdom and warmth of the ages.

Many thanks for reading this book. I hope it gave you as much joy as it did me.

If you would like to contact Charulatha or Team Miblart, their details are as follows:

charu.dpp@gmail.com
team@miblart.com

GLOSSARY OF TERMS

1. Holi Moly!

1. Elder sister
2. Brother (informal)
3. Scarf
4. Long shirt
5. Hindu Spring festival of colour
6. Watchman
7. Is it fixed or not?
8. Long shirt, normally worn by women
9. The heart is still Indian
10. Water gun
11. Indian homespun cotton cloth
12. Flattened rice dish, normally served as breakfast
13. Sweet dessert pudding made from grated carrots
14. Fried bread with potato curry
15. Vegetables coated in seasoned batter and fried
16. Rice and lentil dish
17. Savoury snack made of puffed rice, vegetables and a tangy tamarind sauce
18. Spicy curry and Indian bread roll
19. Long shirt and trousers, normally worn by men
20. Traditional name given to the coloured powders used for the typical Hindu rituals, in particular for the Holi festival.
21. Son
22. A mild preparation of marijuana made from young leaves and stems of the Indian hemp plant
23. Indian sweet made from a mixture of flour, sugar, and shortening, which is shaped into a ball
24. Potato curry

2. An Unsuitable Boy

1. Indian tea made by boiling tea leaves with milk, sugar, and sometimes spices
2. Foreigner
3. Elder sister
4. White
5. A knee-length coat buttoning to the neck

3. Karma-Band

1. Is she yours?
2. Nanny
3. Father's sister/Aunty
4. Baby-term for urine
5. Let's go

4. The Best Laid Plans

1. The general public
2. Indian Subcontinent flat bread, made from stoneground wholemeal flour and lentil curry
3. A food, visually similar to cake and compositionally similar to khaman, made from a batter of gram flour (from chickpeas), cooked by steaming
4. Bring the tea quickly!
5. Bread container
6. A sweet dish made out of khoa and sugar
7. The usually decorated end of a sari that hangs loose when worn
8. Sister (informal), used as a mark of respect
9. Grandfather
10. Mother in Gujarati

5. The Return

1. Kohl, powder for applying to the eyes
2. A light bedstead
3. Fig tree of India noted for great size and longevity
4. Ji: A suffix used as a mark of respect
5. Coins
6. Brother
7. Elder sister
8. An Indian sweet made from milk solids and sugar and typically flavoured with cardamom or nuts
9. An Indian sweet made from a mixture of flour, sugar, and shortening, which is shaped into a ball
10. A landowner, especially one who leases his land to tenant farmers

6. Top That

1. Aunties
2. Grandfather

3. Uncles
4. Fortune-teller
5. Village council
6. Foreigner/ white person (informal)
7. Maize bread and mustard greens - a dish very popular in rural Punjab
8. Clarified butter
9. Solid
10. A vigorous dance
11. Fresh betel leaves wrapped around fruits and nuts, used as a digestive, mild stimulant or mouth freshener
12. A sweet preserve of rose petals
13. Caustic lime
14. Betel nut
15. Paan seller
16. Food
17. A colloquial saying which means "You rich son of a rich father" implying someone who is entitled and spoilt
18. Sweetmeats

7. Funk

1. A maid
2. Hugs

8. Lost And Found

1. Vegetable seller
2. Tea
3. Chit-chat
4. Old man
5. Hand over your money!
6. Son
7. Boys/Children
8. Sweet makers
9. Fireworks
10. Card games

ABOUT THE AUTHOR

A bookworm since childhood, her imagination was channelled into writing by her mother. She won several competitions at school and university for her writing but never pursued it seriously. After several years of a writing hiatus, akin to being in writing Siberia, a competition in a newspaper reignited her love. The outcome was Parvathy's Well.

That story remains special as it once again set her on the path to writing, and reacquainting herself with her dormant creative self.

She lives and works in the United Kingdom, is married and has two teenage daughters.

www.ingramcontent.com/pod-product-compliance
Lightning Source LLC
Chambersburg PA
CBHW031418200726
48285CB00017BA/2424